# The Ghost of a Chance

# The Ghost of a Chance

Krewe of Hunters

By Heather Graham

The Ghost of a Chance
Krewe of Hunters
Copyright 2024 Heather Graham Pozzessere

ISBN: 978-1-968707-59-0

Published by Blue Box Press, an imprint of Evil Eye Concepts, Incorporated

# Dedication

*For Paulette Arthurs with lots and lots—and lots of thanks!*

# Prologue

David Clancy knew what was happening; he saw it all clearly as it began.

He just didn't know what in God's name he could do to stop it.

He saw the guns. He saw the people in the bank. Ordinary people. Out and about on their daily business—mothers, fathers, sisters, brothers, friends…children. Just people. And he knew how dangerous everything about to happen might be.

He knew all too well.

The glass part of the wall in front of the bank was tinted, but he could still see what was going on. He saw that someone had been ordered to collect all the phones.

He saw the tellers being ordered to come around from behind their stations and determined that one of them had been culled to collect the cell phones, certainly promising death to anyone who disobeyed the order.

He knew too well…

And he had to help.

How? How would he help? He couldn't do a damn thing to the robbers wielding the guns.

A feeling of desperation grew within him, and his powerlessness was infuriating. There had to be *something* he could do.

Whatever it was, he couldn't do it from outside the bank.

But he could slip in unnoticed.

There were certain benefits to being long dead.

He could slip right through the glass and not alarm anyone in the least.

# Chapter 1

Billy Mendelson had the nose of his Glock 18 pressed tightly to Angela's temple. She knew the gun.

She knew its capabilities.

What she didn't understand was how a young man who had graduated with honors and attended a prestigious college on a full scholarship could be standing there, gun pressed to her head, threatening the staff, customers, and three little children in the bank with certain death if they didn't follow his every instruction.

Except, when she realized who he was, she also remembered what had happened to him.

He'd already warned that if an alarm went off in any way, shape, or form, he'd shoot her and move on to the children.

Being a member of the FBI's specialized unit known as the Krewe of Hunters, Angela Hawkins Crow was familiar with guns—and very bad situations.

Billy smiled at her. "Right now, lady, you're it. If anything goes wrong…"

"I don't believe anything will go wrong. And I can help you," Angela told him.

While years of experience might help her deal with her

physical and verbal reactions to a situation, she was human. And she couldn't help but think about her children: Corby, who was managing his final years of high school with excellence. And Victoria, who was now into gymnastics, dance, and swimming…

She thought of Jackson, head of the Krewe. Also, husband, father, companion, and partner in all from the beginning. The love of her life…

And the Krewe itself, even the people working in the Blackbird Division. They called her when they needed help. She'd become an amazing expert at finding information on just about anything…

*No one is irreplaceable*, she reminded herself.

But she didn't want to be replaced.

And then there was the physical death, of course. Well, if he shot her at this range and from this angle, it would at least be quick: intense pain for seconds, perhaps, but then…

"Billy. Please," she said quietly. "We will do whatever you say. There's no reason for anyone to die here."

"No?" he asked her. "Well, people die. Death is a fact of life."

He was a handsome young man, tall with a good thatch of dark hair cut so a lock fell over his forehead. He was green-eyed and possessed good, strong cheekbones.

A woman huddled on the floor by the tellers' stand suddenly cried out.

"How can you do this? After—"

Billy, holding Angela with the nose of the gun still held tight to her head, swung around to stare at her.

"You can go first," he told her. "Like I said, people die."

People did die. As he'd said, death was a fact of life. But Angela remembered the event she had seen and read in the news, an event the Krewe of Hunters hadn't had any involvement in. It had been a hard investigation.

And never solved.

*Mendelson.*

Just weeks ago, robbers had broken into the house of a jewelry designer and his wife, killing the couple and getting away with a small fortune in diamonds.

The couple was this young man's parents. So, knowing that pain, how could he?

"Billy. You said you wanted us in the vault. Just put us all in there and do whatever you need to do. Please," Angela said. "We're not stupid. We'll do whatever you want us to do. No alarms, no police."

A little boy sitting on the floor with his mother, perhaps five or six years old, began to sniffle and cry.

"Shut him up!" Billy warned.

"Please. Just get us all into the vault, just as you said you wanted to do. Then take whatever you want," Angela said again, careful to speak softly but clearly, offering a smile that wasn't at all filled with laughter but did contain warmth.

One thing her years with the bureau had given her were classes in self-defense, negotiations, and profiling…

Classes that taught her when self-defense was an option, the best way to speak during negotiations, and how to deal with someone who was so badly on the edge that every single care had to be taken to keep oneself or a roomful of people from being killed.

Of course, she could only pray that she was putting the pieces together properly.

"Please," she repeated. "We will all do every single thing you tell us to do."

He whispered something, but she barely heard him.

"I'm sorry."

He moved closer to her as if his words were meant only for her.

"My mother did that—everything those bastards said.

And they killed her and my dad anyway."

"But that's them, Billy. Not you," she told him. Her words were almost a whisper now. This had come to something that was between the two of them.

"You know who I am."

"And my heart bleeds for you. Billy, I know you probably won't believe this, but I can help you. I can employ every resource in the world to trap the monsters who hurt your parents," she told him. "Really—"

"The cops were all over it."

"Not to brag, but I'm almost a genius with the Internet. I can find out what others can't. And I have friends who are just as good."

"No, no, no. I'll be gone to the moon—well, South America, at least. Somewhere far, far, away. And I'll start over completely. Or I'll be dead," he told her.

"Then we'll get everyone into the vault now, and when you're gone, I'll still try to find justice for your parents," she vowed.

He looked at her for a long moment, and she thought maybe he believed her. Right now, there was only one objective: to keep these people alive.

And she would do anything in the world to make that happen, praying that, somehow, she might keep herself alive, as well. There might be one problem, though. Jackson and Corby knew where she was. She had simply run to the bank to pull out some cash for Corby's class's fundraiser for the victims of the latest storm that had wiped out hundreds of homes. They'd planned on buying pastries created by all the kids' different parents and turning their purchases into an impromptu party for those in the Krewe who were in the area at the moment.

Billy smiled suddenly. "You'd best all behave," he told her. "Because I'm not alone. Say hi, Kenneth."

At the front of the bank, one of the men seated on the floor waved a hand in the air and rose, reaching beneath his jacket as he did.

He, too, had a gun. From her distance, Angela couldn't tell what type of handgun it might be.

But regardless, it carried bullets and death.

Her family knew she was here. And while she had incredible faith in Jackson, she prayed he was able to control the situation, and that no one barged in, guns blazing.

Because that would surely cause a bloodbath.

———————••••———————

"Where's Mom?" Corby asked Jackson. "She's usually faster than a speeding bullet. Oh, sorry, Dad, I guess comparisons to bullets isn't a great thing in your line of work."

Jackson made a face for his son. "Maybe the bank was busy. I should have told her to just use the ATM."

"You know Mom. She probably wanted more cash than she could pull from the machine. When she says we're buying stuff from everybody, she means *everybody*," Corby said and laughed softly. "And she may be worrying about paying for her own pastries—she isn't sure everyone will like her eclairs."

"Hey, I worked on those eclairs, too," Jackson reminded him.

"Maybe that's what she's afraid of," Corby teased.

"Stop picking on Mommy," Victoria demanded, standing to her full height.

Jackson grinned. Corby was their adopted son. They had met years ago on a very strange case where they discovered that the very young-at-the-time Corby needed parents—and that he had their special talent…or curse, as well. Then they had Victoria. They were truly blessed because their kids loved each other.

Even though they were part of a unit that dealt with the very worst of human depravity far too often, their family made it work. And they got to see the best in humanity, as well.

Corby made a face. "I'm just…" He paused and looked at Jackson. Jackson knew his son didn't want to say that he was worried and make his sister worried, as well.

"All right. Corby, take your sister—and the eclairs— down to the tables outside the store. I'll head to the bank and find out what's going on with Mom. I'll also call Mrs. Cunningham, your friend Justin's mom, and ask her to—" He paused. He had a lot of faith in his son, but Corby was still a kid. Still, he didn't want to use the words *look out for you.*

"To help you if you need anything," Jackson finished.

"You mean you want her to look after us," Corby said.

Jackson groaned. "Whatever. Go. I'll see what's up."

Corby grinned. "Yes, sir," he told his father. "Victoria, let's head out."

The two walked in one direction while Jackson headed in the other to the bank. As he neared it, he slowed his pace. He wasn't sure how he knew, but he just *knew* something was wrong. There was a note on the door.

*Reopening at 2:00. Computer failure.*

Computers could glitch, but at the same time, such a message on the door seemed a little odd.

Jackson moved carefully, sliding against the wall at a distance, then easing along it to a point where he could see through the tinted glass.

There were people in the bank.

On the floor.

Well, the note allowed for a new kind of holdup. Maybe the bank robbers just wanted the money and had no desire to kill anyone.

But among those in the bank, someone would want to be a hero, this was a situation where heroes could get others killed.

He didn't dare call Angela and alert a possible killer, though it might not matter. The robbers had probably collected everyone's cell phones first thing.

He needed eyes and ears in the place, and while his team could move within minutes, they might not have even that long.

Jackson saw Angela and a young man at her side.

One with a gun to her head.

But it looked like Angela was speaking to him. It was difficult to see clearly beyond the tint in the glass.

He slipped farther back to make sure he wasn't seen and pulled out his phone to call for backup.

---

"Please let me get everyone into the vault," Angela pleaded, keeping her voice sweet. "I can do this with everyone behaving perfectly. And then you'll have us out of the way, and you and Kenneth can clean out the cashiers' stations and get everything you want."

"How do you know what I want?"

"You are committing armed robbery in a bank. That should mean you want money," Angela said, still keeping her voice as sweet as possible. "I'm ready to help you toward that goal."

"Why?"

"Because you can get your money, and then you and Kenneth can get away," Angela said. "I'm sure Kenneth wants the cash. That's why he's using you and your pain to help him," she added as if reasoning it all out in her mind.

Billy frowned. For a moment, Angela was afraid she

might have pushed the wrong button. But in the boy's frown, she saw that she was right. Kenneth—whoever he was—had pounced upon the young man's pain. Billy was being used.

"All right," Billy announced loudly.

The gun was no longer pointed at Angela's temple; instead, he had aimed it at the crowd.

For split seconds, Angela considered making a calculated lunge, but a trigger could be pulled so quickly that, despite all the training in the world, such a tactic could fail.

"This lady is going to direct you all to the vault. You follow her, or you die."

There was one problem, of course. Angela couldn't open the vault.

She stepped forward. "I need the bank manager. This place *is* going to be robbed," she said, "but we can all live. Please, help me."

A slim, attractive woman with light-auburn hair stepped forward. She appeared to be in her late thirties or early forties and seemed nervous but determined.

"I'm Elise Benton," she said. "The main manager is off today. I'm his assistant."

Angela nodded gravely to her, giving her a grim smile that showed her thanks.

"Then, Ms. Benton, you'll lead the people, and I'll follow to make sure we all get in safely," Angela said.

"How adorable," the man Billy had called Kenneth quipped.

Angela observed him carefully. He looked to be in his mid to late thirties, so he had almost twenty years on Billy. He stood to about five-ten and had a medium build, longish blond hair, and a clean-shaven face. But something about his expression was hard, as if he didn't care one way or another if anyone died. Maybe he was unhappy that it didn't appear they were going to shoot someone. It didn't look like anyone in the bank would give them any trouble.

Not even the two guards. They'd emptied and tossed their guns when they first saw Billy aiming his weapon at a boy of about ten.

Angela tried to count people as they passed. The bank tellers, the manager, and two young women who had been working at their desks totaled six. Two guards, seven adult customers, and three children—aged five years to ten, if she had to guess.

"Follow me, please," Elise Benton said.

"What if we want something that's in the vault?" Kenneth asked Billy.

"Um, no one can open the private boxes," Elise told him.

"No. The other vault. Where you keep the real money," Kenneth said.

"I will open it," Elise promised. "I will open it for you, I swear."

"You need to tell Elise what you want done," Angela explained. "Do you want her to open the money vault and have you lock her in the vault with all the personal boxes?"

"Kenneth," Billy called. "Come over here. Take Elise to open the rear vault. No, wait. Open the first one so we can get the others in, and *then* take her on down to the rear as soon as you get the first open for them to start getting in."

Apparently, Billy and Kenneth knew the setup at the bank.

Angela and Jackson had been doing their banking here forever. They had a safety deposit box here themselves. There wasn't much of worth in it except to them and their kids. They had papers about their family history and impor-tant information should something happen to them, legal documents—critical in their line of work—and a few bits and pieces that weren't expensive but mattered to them as they had belonged to their families and were old.

Their things in their little box in the vault didn't matter. But it meant Angela knew the bank's layout. The front had the teller stations and a few desks for those with other banking business. A hall to the right when you faced the street led to the restrooms, the break room, the manager's office, the vault with the customer's boxes, and lastly, the vault with the bank's supply of cash. There was a back door that led out to open employee parking in the back, but during office hours, it automatically locked—Angela had learned that while chatting with the manager once.

It was a safety precaution.

An alarm could be triggered by the manager or any of the tellers, but the manager had already come out of her office to speak with one of the desk officers when Billy announced the holdup, saying he'd shoot a teller and a customer if any alarms went off.

*No help from the back*, Angela thought dryly. Because if someone tried to breach the bank that way, an alarm *would* go off.

Despite his threats, she wasn't sure about Billy.

Somewhere inside him was the boy who had watched his parents' murders. Who had felt the agony of losing them before his very eyes.

But Kenneth…

He was a long shot. He seemed amused by the terror around him.

They paused for Elise to go through the numbers on the vault and let the sensor scan her eye.

The door opened, and people filed in, two moms and one dad urging their children inside quickly. The bank employees, including the two security guards, went last.

One of the guards paused and looked at Angela. There was something hopeless in his eyes, as if he felt he had failed them all. She shook her head briefly, wishing she could tell him he'd done the right thing by giving up his weapon. If he'd tried to stop these two, he and someone else would have likely died.

"Right. See, everyone is getting into the vault," Angela said to Billy.

"Yeah, yeah. Your people are walking in," Billy said.

"Like I said," she told him softly.

"Right."

"Move. I need to go on with this, er, lady," Kenneth said.

"Go on," Billy told him. "We're out of the way."

"She can help with the cases. Get them all filled up," Kenneth said, pointing at Angela. He grimaced and went on with Elise to the far vault.

Billy looked at Angela.

"Not you," he said. "You're helping with the cases."

"I can't open anything here," she told him. "I'm just a customer—"

"We need help filling our bags with the money."

"I will do whatever you need."

He smiled. "Right. And you'll make a great human shield if anyone gets in here and tries to shoot Ken or me."

# Chapter 2

Naturally, Jackson had reported the incident to the head of the bureau, letting him manage cooperation with other law enforcement. Still, he knew the man would see to it that others were kept at a distance, ready to step in when necessary.

He had determined that only a small number of his unit would join him at the bank.

Because once the group disappeared down the hall to the vaults, he couldn't see them anymore.

He couldn't see Angela.

He'd never met a better person at assessing a situation and determining how to best play any essential tactics than his wife.

He had faith.

But faith didn't completely alleviate fear.

He knew about the back door. He also knew that when it was locked during business hours or at night, an alarm would go off if it was breached in any way.

Thus, as the group disappeared down the hallway, he stood where he had been, trying to weigh the possibilities.

As he did, a man approached the front door, tried it,

read the sign, and then swore in frustration before moving on.

"They even take closing breaks during the day at banks now. Computer, my ass."

The irritated man moved on down the street.

If there was just some form of communication…

But he knew that whoever was in there had a gun. He also knew that Angela would try to keep everyone as calm as possible—making saving human lives paramount over money. It would help if he knew how many gunmen there were. Or would it?

He'd been with the bureau for a long time—the longest as a special supervisory agent for the Krewe. Life was the only resource that couldn't be replaced. But in his years in law enforcement, he'd seen cases where killers murdered victims for the fun of it or just because they sneezed too loudly.

So…

"Sir?"

Hearing the softly spoken address, Jackson turned. A man was at his side—a tall one of mixed race, handsome, and wearing a suit that appeared a little outdated. His face was strongly chiseled: high cheekbones, strong chin, and dark eyes set below a high brow. His vest suggested something from the Victorian era, especially considering the tailed jacket and puff of white shirt beneath it.

And then he realized the man was dead. He had been approached by a ghost.

His breath caught. Help! The kind he needed.

"Sir, hello, yes. I'm Jackson Crow—"

"And you see me," the man exclaimed happily. "Dear God, I feared I'd be here, see what was going on, and… A man can go years without finding a seer such as yourself. I didn't know what I could possibly do… And now I'm rambling, and the situation is dire. David Clancy, sir. Captain

David Clancy. Signed up after the Second Confiscation and Militia Act of July 1862."

"Thank you, Captain," Jackson said. "For now, and for your service. You've been in the bank?" he asked.

The ghost of David Clancy nodded gravely. "There is a young woman in there, a beautiful blonde, who is doing the majority of the talking. She's convinced the robbers to get the people into the vault that holds the customers' boxes while taking the assistant manager to retrieve the money from the cash vault. I watched and then noticed you and the way you were moving. I'd tried to approach others for help—got a few shivers from a couple of them—but not a seer among them. You looked like some type of officer, so I thought I couldn't lose by taking another chance."

"We need to hurry. Except—"

"Except," David Clancy said grimly, "if you burst in there, someone will start shooting, and children might die. The robbers are…well, one of them is a total mystery. I thought he was the *brains*, so to say, but now I think the other was the impetus behind everything going on and brainwashed the kid into doing this."

"Kid?" Jackson asked. He had help now. He could truly assess the situation.

"Appears to be about seventeen or eighteen. The blonde called him Billy, and I remembered something about a home robbery not long ago where some folks were killed in front of their son. I think that's the boy. The woman has a rapport going with him."

"Angela," Jackson whispered. "She would."

"You know her, sir?"

"She's my wife. And an agent, as well. We're with the Federal Bureau of Investigation. It's an agency—"

"Sir—"

"Call me Jackson, please."

"David," the ghost said politely. "I know about the world today. One thing about wandering the Earth is that you get to see and hear a great deal. I know this is all expedient. And I'd be rushing more, except people will die if you burst in."

"That's been my dilemma," Jackson told him.

"But I know another way," David said.

Jackson frowned. "There's a back door. We bank here, which is, of course, why my wife Angela is in there. But the back door is uber-alarmed. It's a small branch of a major bank, so the security measures—"

"Are meant to save the facility more than the people," David commented dryly.

Jackson nodded. "So?"

"That's not the only way in that I know about," David said and appeared to inhale. "Once upon a time, tunnels extended all down the street—part of the Underground Railroad. When I was a child, I came through them with my mother. We had friends in DC waiting for us. As I mentioned, I signed up when I could."

Jackson hesitated. He had served himself. Still, he winced as he asked, "And you…?"

"Oh, no, I wasn't killed in the war. I was nineteen in 1862. I made it into the twentieth century. I saw some of the worst days of human carnage possible, but I also learned that any man can be a good man, and any woman can be mean or kind. I watched generations of my family grow. And that is why I know that a tunnel with an entrance to the bank through a supply closet in the assistant manager's office remains. One of my grandsons held the job until he passed of natural causes several years back."

Jackson looked at David and nodded.

All the souls who remained had stories. The captain's seemed to have a harsh beginning but a good ending.

Unfortunately, they couldn't get into it now.

"How do we get into the tunnel?" he asked David.

"The sewer."

"Why doesn't everyone know about the entrance?" Jackson asked.

"Because you have to know where the old break in the stretch leads to another old break in the stretch. Not that many people like to play in the sewers," David said dryly.

"Yes, but the workers—"

David shrugged. "I'm sure some know there are holes that lead to holes. But mostly, they're down there to work—and get the hell out. Where we're going anyway. You ready?"

"We can come up in the assistant manager's office?" Jackson asked, wanting the assurance.

"Yes. And no one working there now knows that the shelving unit to the left of the desk slides open. I don't think anyone has known for the last forty years or so," David told him.

"I'm ready to get dirty," Jackson said. "I just need a minute to tell one of my senior agents so he keeps our backup out of sight and controls anyone else."

"You are armed, right?" David said.

"Oh, yeah. But I'm hoping…"

"Angela, your wife, the blonde in the bank. You're hoping she can bring about a happy ending?"

"Exactly."

"Then wouldn't it make sense to let them steal whatever they want and leave the bank?"

"It would, except they'll be prepared. They'll bring a few human shields when they come out and…well, if we have to take someone out, we need to do it with an element of surprise."

David nodded grimly. "It's an honor to work with you, sir," he said.

"No, Captain. It's an honor to work with *you*," Jackson assured him.

He called Bruce McFadden, who often stood in for him, and gave him command of whatever happened on the outside.

Then David was ready to lead the way. In a few minutes, he was casually watching the street…

And then following the ghost into the sewer.

He hopped through the lifted grate and hit the ground. The smell was overwhelming. The ancient walls were covered with a damp slime, and the ground beneath his feet was filled with God alone knew what.

And then it *covered* his feet.

And then his ankles.

Into it up to his knees, he trudged through with Captain Clancy, wincing and thinking that it had to be easier getting through certain situations as a ghost.

Yet he didn't care if he had to roll in the sewer. Not only was it his job—his vocation—to stop violent criminals and save the innocent, but there was also no way out of human emotion.

His wife was in that bank. He had tremendous faith and belief in her and had seen her manage situations that might have been impossible for anyone else—himself included.

Still…

He had to get her out.

------------·••·------------

"Everyone is in," Angela said. "Where are we getting these bags you're talking about that we'll need to fill up with the money?"

"Front of the bank," Billy told her. "Let's go."

"As you command," she assured him.

The door to the vault with the personal boxes was locked at the moment, and the people in there were safe.

Elise wasn't so safe, but Angela couldn't see or help the woman. The best she could do was try to draw Billy out and discover if there was any way to reason with him. Understand him…

Make him turn on Kenneth.

"Front of the bank," Billy said again. "And I've still got the gun. I can shoot you if you so much as blink, so don't give me any trouble."

"I don't intend to give you any trouble," she assured him. "I will do everything you order me to do. You have the people in the vault, and I believe you intend to leave them there. But…"

"But what?"

She shook her head. "I…I don't know about Kenneth. I mean, I know what happened to you, Billy. And I must admit, I don't understand this. You were so unfairly and brutally hurt. Your pain must be far beyond agonizing. But you were an incredible student and, more, an incredible human being. While awful, I just don't believe it turned you so drastically, making you want to hurt people. Kill people. Put others in the same horrendous state of anguish and pain you were in. Children. Especially children—"

"I don't want to hurt any kids," he snapped at her.

"No, of course you don't," she murmured.

She might have pushed too hard. She glanced back at him as he propelled her toward the front of the bank.

"The cases are—?"

"Just ahead. Two little suitcases, roller cases, the kind you can stuff in the overhead of an airplane," he told her. "Right there."

"I see them," she assured him, heading for the luggage.

They were just inside the bank's entrance.

She saw that the sign warning that the bank would soon reopen was still up. But of course it was. While it seemed like a lifetime ago, it had only been ten minutes or so since Billy and Kenneth came into the bank. Billy had started the holdup by aiming his gun at one of the kids and warning that if his every word wasn't followed, a child would die.

And then as many other people as he could hit before being taken down himself.

And Angela was glad—so, *so* glad—that the guards had chosen not to be heroes. They hadn't even known about Kenneth at first. But between them, he and Billy could have mown down just about everyone in the bank before going down themselves.

Still, as she pretended to study the cases, Angela did her best to peer through the tinted windows.

Jackson knew by now that something was wrong. She prayed he wouldn't come to the bank with their children.

Of course, he wouldn't. Jackson was too smart for that. He was too smart to threaten anyone until he knew the situation. But how could he possibly know?

But he did. She knew it. He knew what was going on. She didn't see him, but she *did* see Bruce McFadden. He leaned against a telephone pole outside, on his cell, laughing and chatting as if he had just stopped on the street to make a call.

That meant Jackson knew and understood what was going on. He would weigh every option and make sure the local police didn't barge in and risk the lives of the hostages as they maintained control of the situation.

"Here. I've got them. Let's go get them all filled up with money," she said.

She turned back to look at Billy. He still had his gun aimed at her, but he was staring off into space.

Suddenly, he began to talk—perhaps to himself, her, or

maybe the universe.

"She never did anything to anyone. She was one of the best human beings to ever live. And they just shot her down while laughing. They thought it was funny to see the terror in her eyes, to make me watch… And my father? He begged and begged. He didn't care about himself. He just wanted them to let my mother go and not kill me. And the bastard told them not to worry. Said he wouldn't hurt me. That he wanted to let me live because it would screw me all up. Because the world wasn't fair. Everyone expects it to be fair, and it just isn't."

Billy suddenly turned to look at Angela. "That's the whole thing, you see. It isn't fair. But our minister said my parents were beautiful people. And told me I would see them again. Because, surely, if they were such good people, I'd see them again in Heaven. They were fair and equal. They loved everybody."

"I can tell you this because I have children," Angela said. "Your parents are happy in Heaven. It didn't matter what that monster did to them as long as they left you alive. They *were* beautiful people. You should be following in all they taught—"

"No. Beautiful people get screwed," he told her. "That's what I've learned. It's the monsters in the world who survive," he said angrily.

"The odd thing is that you're saying those words, yet I don't think you believe them. I think you are a product of your parents. You are a beautiful person, too—"

"Beautiful people die," he told her.

"Not always. And often, oh so often, monsters wind up being put down. Trust me. If they don't die, they spend the rest of their lives in prison and behind bars. I've seen it so many times," Angela told him.

He started to laugh. "What? On television?"

Angela shook her head and looked at him. "No, Billy. In real life. Monsters very often wind up where they should be. In cages."

He seemed to give himself a mental shake that extended to a bit of a twitch in his face.

"Get the cases. We need to get them back to the vault, or Kenneth will come out and shoot you before we get anywhere."

"Kenneth will shoot me?" she asked. "Not you?" She almost whispered it.

"I will shoot you if I have to," he assured her.

"But you don't want to," she said softly.

"I just said that I *will* shoot you if I have to," Billy insisted.

"But again, you don't want to. A guy like Kenneth, however…he's just itching to shoot someone. So far, you've kept him from doing so. I've been trying to keep these people alive, but you're the one who has been doing it. You're trying to keep everyone safe from Kenneth."

"Pick up those cases, or I *will* shoot you," Billy thundered.

"Just do as he says. Help is on the way. The right kind of help."

Angela tried not to react to the words in any way.

Because they hadn't been spoken by anyone living.

Looking beyond Billy toward the assistant manager's office, Angela could see a man. He was tall and well-built, with dark eyes and heavily graying dark hair—a striking man in a suit with a strong face.

A suit from a different age.

A ghost. A ghost was here to help them.

Which meant they now had a ghost of a chance.

# Chapter 3

Jackson understood how people could work in the sewers and not know about the sewer tunnels built to use the deep channels in the earth that had long ago been part of the Underground Railroad.

Time—and waste matter—could do a number on the earth, no matter what.

But down here…

Well, the captain was right. They had followed a main line for about a block. Then there was a small break in the wall—one Jackson had barely managed to squeeze through. That had led to an overflow tunnel.

And the fetid water had risen past his waist.

But then they reached a hole in the old wall. Jackson had to hold his breath and soak himself to get through it, but then David pointed.

A slope led upward, and there was no water at what appeared to be the top—and solid roofing.

"There," David had told him. "It's been years—years and years—since anyone tried to get through. But these days, it just looks like shelves built into the wall on the other side. You'll have to push hard and then hike yourself up into the space. There's a small opening, like a supply closet, that will take you behind the bottom of the office shelving." He paused, studying Jackson. "You look like you can manage it. I want to go ahead. That way, I'll know what's happening now, and if…"

*If anyone has been killed.*

"It's a good plan, David, thank you. You need to know, Angela will be able to see you. I need you to tell her to keep playing it the way she's been doing. That help is on the way. She'll understand you've reached me or another Krewe member—"

"Krewe?" David said, sounding puzzled and a bit worried.

Jackson shook his head. "It's the professional title for our unit of the FBI. According to most people, we're the ones sent in whenever something about a case hints at the occult, witchcraft, or anything strange. Some of the other agents call us the *ghostbusters*. Our scientists have figured out that it's a genetic talent in only about two percent of the population. We can see the souls who have remained on Earth for whatever reason, whenever they want to be seen."

"Ah. So…yes. That makes so much sense," David said. "Some people shiver, and some—through the decades—have seen me. I tried earlier. I tried and tried until I found you. I guess I found the right person. But I wonder if…"

"Yes?"

David smiled and shook his head. "I wonder if that's why I'm still here. I've seen others go. I wasn't murdered, my descendants have lived good lives, and…well, I'm still here. But we'll talk later. Let me get up there and talk to Angela."

"Go. I'm right behind you," Jackson said. "And I'm in decent shape—it's required for my job. I should be able to manage the physical part of it, but then we'll have to figure out the best way for me to proceed once I'm in there."

"I'm gone," David told him.

And he was.

Jackson continued through the sludge.

He hesitated once, noting there were two ragged holes in the wall. He knew which way he was going, yet he couldn't help but allow a few seconds of curiosity as he regarded the other hole.

Where did it lead?

It was stygian within, yet he couldn't help but notice that his phone's light seemed to glint off something white.

Like bone.

Maybe he'd been doing his job for too long.

He forged on, heading up the ramp that led to the old entrance to the bank from the tunnels.

Once upon a time, the bank had probably been something else. Maybe a home, a business, or someplace else where those who had escaped slavery could enter the world and become masters of their own destinies. It was something the world continued to work on to this day.

Time did a number on all things. Jackson struggled to see just where the latch to the secret entrance might be. When he discovered and pulled on it, it left him in dismay.

Even metal rotted and gave way with time.

But he could see where the opening was supposed to be and wedge his fingers into a tiny gap.

And…

He looked around at the residue of soot and…other stuff…left behind when the water rose and receded and found a couple of pebbles.

He got them wedged in and pressed and pulled, warning himself not to waste his energy on frustration but to keep trying, seeking…

Life itself might depend on his ability to gain entrance.

Angela was good.

But no matter how good she was, she might fail if someone in the bank wasn't there for the money but because they were excited by the prospect of a kill.

He forced himself to be calm and work at what he was doing.

Finally...*finally*...

The ancient wood began to give way. It broke apart and fell around him.

But that didn't matter.

He pushed with all his strength against the modern wood paneling within the office and felt it suddenly give way.

After all, it had been built against an ancient trap door, leading to what once might have been the unknown, except to those who had so desperately created the tunnel, the doors, and the path to freedom.

Maybe, just maybe, history and time had created a path for him to the incredible freedom of life itself.

But he had to be careful. Careful and quiet. He managed to slide his legs through the opening, grip with his calves and hands, and hike himself up. He understood how no one in the office knew about the strange entrance into what was now the bowels of the sewer. Once opened, it was little more than a cubby at the base of the floor behind the shelving, covered until he had broken the old latch, the wood, and the insulation.

But now he was in the assistant manager's office. He had managed to get in without sounding the alarm.

He stood still, listening. Nothing. Of course, he didn't know where those who had been in the bank were now.

David would find him here and give him an update.

Now...

He just had to hope his stink wouldn't alert anyone to his presence.

David came in as Jackson surveyed the room, contemplating his next move.

"I know you can't speak out loud, but I'm decent at lip reading," the ghost assured him. "At this moment, everyone is all right. The people—including the guards—are in the safety deposit box vault. Angela is in the back with Billy Mendelson, packing bags with the *right* bills. Apparently, Kenneth wants twenties and fifties, and none with sequential serial numbers."

"*What is this Kenneth doing?*" Jackson mouthed.

"Watching. Just watching. He has the gun. Billy isn't armed right now. He's working with Angela to get the proper bills he wants to steal into the suitcases. When I first entered…" David paused, frowning.

"What?" Jackson whispered.

"He was on his cell phone."

"A burner phone, I'm sure," Jackson murmured.

David shrugged. "It can't be just the two of them. There must be someone outside waiting. Maybe with a getaway vehicle—a car, van…truck. Probably a car. Something that can disappear into traffic."

Jackson nodded, indicating for David to watch the door. He moved to the back of the office, the farthest from the door, and dialed Bruce McFadden.

Bruce answered immediately. "Standing by a pole across the street," Bruce told him. "Everyone's aware that hostages' lives are at stake. They've given our unit lead, but we have the local police out here, too. Nicely scattered. No one is obvious."

"Good. I'm in," Jackson told him. "And a friend is in here with me—a great guy you'll need to meet. He's reporting to me on what's happening. He said he believes there has to be a third person—or maybe even a couple of people— involved in this on the outside. Someone ready to take off when they finish the robbery."

"My eyes are open. And Will Chan and Kat are in the rear. They're pretending to be on a date, enjoying shakes while sitting on the hood of a car just outside that ice cream shop down the street. If there's a getaway car in the back, they'll see it, and patrol will get a roadblock going," Bruce told him, then hesitated. "You haven't been able to get to Angela yet?" he asked.

"David is watching her—the guy I mentioned," Jackson told him.

"And," Bruce added quickly, "she knows what she's doing."

"Right," Jackson agreed. He took a breath and glanced at Captain Clancy's ghost. The man vigilantly watched the door, and Jackson found himself wishing he had known him in life. He must have been a force: a strong man against the odds of his time, but one who fought for those who needed help and was kind to the innocent.

Jackson made a decision. He had to lure Kenneth to the office.

And make him disappear.

He wondered dryly if his smell alone was enough to kill.

---

Angela heard the tapping sound that seemed to be coming from the front of the bank.

But it wasn't like someone knocking on a door.

It sounded like drapery moving in the wind, or as if something caught on a cord had slipped or fallen and was just lightly tapping against a desk or a floor or something.

She kept at her task, sorting cash as she had been directed, taking the piles that Billy approved of and setting them in one of the cases.

Kenneth had been keeping a close eye on her.

And his gun was still aimed her way.

Almost as if daring her, Billy had set his weapon down, but he'd done it near the door.

Near Kenneth.

Naturally, both Billy and Kenneth heard the sound. Billy paused and stared at Kenneth with a frown.

"What is that?"

Kenneth shook his head. "Probably nothing."

"And we're certain no one has tried to get in yet?" Billy asked him.

"Hey, we're not the only eyes on the place," Kenneth said. "No one is trying to get in. A few people have come by, but walked away when they saw the sign. They'll find another branch."

"But we need to hurry. We need to get out—"

"Fill the cases. Remember, no new currency, no easily traced serial numbers, and no big bills," Kenneth snapped.

"Move faster!" Billy yelled at Angela.

"I'm trying," she assured him.

The tapping noise had stopped. Then, it started up again.

"What in the hell is that?" Billy demanded.

"Nothing, just a dangling cord or some shit," Kenneth snapped back at him. "Get your gun. Watch her. I'll check it out."

Billy did as he'd been ordered. He picked up his weapon and aimed it at Angela.

Kenneth left them, walking the hall and pausing by the vault with the boxes to make sure everything was secure before moving toward the offices at the front of the bank.

They saw him step into a room.

"Billy," Angela said quietly, "you know this bank—or your friend Kenneth does. There's one door in front and one in back. And if anyone touches either of them, an alarm goes off. Thank God no one has tried anything. You two can get your money and get out—"

"With you. You do realize that, right?" Billy asked her.

"If I'm a human shield, then so be it," she said.

"You're awfully accepting. But you know, this is a bank, not a home. People value money way more than they do human life. If the cops come after us, it won't be me who shoots you. It will likely be a cop."

"I'm going on faith, Billy. I'm going to believe that we'll leave here and drive away. And when we're far enough away—"

"We'll let you go? Is that what you're thinking?" he asked her.

"Why wouldn't you?" Angela asked him.

"Oh, come on. You can't be that naïve. You can tell the cops what we look like—you can even tell them who I am."

She might have pointed out that everyone in the bank could probably do that, but there was no sense in putting the other hostages in any worse danger than they were already in.

"I won't tell."

"Don't you watch TV? Everyone says that—in every crime show known to man. And they never mean a word of it."

"Okay." She put the money she'd been gathering back on the table.

"What are you doing? Hurry it up!"

"Why? If you're going to kill me anyway, why should I help you?"

He frowned for a minute and waved the gun at her. "Hope," he snapped, then shook his head, his voice a bit broken when he added, "hope. Don't you think I *hoped* that someone would come and save my parents until the very last minute? I mean, that's only human, right? You hope something will happen, and that maybe, just maybe, you'll be saved."

She stared at him, trying to keep him distracted.

She knew something now that he didn't.

She had help. Jackson knew exactly what was going on. She knew her husband and partner. He'd realize they'd be risking the lives of everyone in the place if they burst in with guns blazing.

He was planning something.

And she knew they also had help that Billy and Kenneth couldn't even begin to imagine. She didn't know who the strange ghost was, but she knew he was helping them.

*Keep packing money!* she told herself. *Keep at it, keep at it.*

She picked up another pile.

"You know, Kenneth was right. That note on the door was brilliant. I mean, everyone knows computers can have glitches. And, boy, when they do… They can really mess things up. The note was smart. People might be aggravated because they just wanted to run into the bank, but they'll believe the note. You know that whole thing…technology is great. When it works."

"Yeah, that's Kenneth," Billy muttered. "Flippin' genius."

He looked down the hall.

Angela couldn't see what was going on, but since Billy was looking, she thought maybe he could see Kenneth—see where he was, what he was doing.

"I guess he checked the front," Angela said. "But seriously, I mean, think about it. People see the sign and walk away. We all know there's a front and a back door, and both doors have major alarms if anyone tries to jimmy them."

Billy shivered suddenly as if a cold blast of wind had hit him.

Angela quickly realized it wasn't wind. Billy Mendelson had what they referred to at the Krewe as sensitivity. He couldn't see or speak with the dead, but he got enough strange senses to know when a spirit was around.

The tall, handsome man in what appeared to be Victorian dress, had come down the hallway, entered the room, and walked right by Billy, thus giving the boy that strange shiver.

"We need to get out of here," Billy snapped. "Get going with the money. Come on. Please, hurry. Look, I really don't want you dead. But Kenneth *will* kill you. We need to get out of here and safely. If we can get far enough away, make the right connections…maybe, just maybe I can figure out a way for you to live."

"I'm hurrying," Angela said, frowning slightly at the ghost, making a pretense of working with the money as she looked at him, waiting for him to speak.

"It's Jackson," the ghost told her. "Jackson is in here. And he's trying to lure Kenneth to him. Hopefully…well, right now, the guy is wandering around, searching for the sound. But I believe there will be a way… I believe Jackson will get Kenneth. But he wanted you to know what was going on so you'd be prepared."

She nodded slightly and quickly asked Billy, "You are a good man, Billy. You've had a brilliant past. Yes, you dealt with unimaginable pain, but this isn't you. How on earth did you wind up with a monster like Kenneth?"

"You don't understand. You'd never understand," Billy said.

"I'd like to try," Angela told him.

He shook his head. "People like Kenneth…even when you do what they say, you may not live." He looked straight at her. "It's a miracle you got him to let those people live by locking them in the vault."

"No one fought him. No one was doing anything but obeying him," Angela said. "I take it he really wants all this money. I assume you plan on heading out to an island somewhere, or a country without extradition to the United

States," Angela said.

Billy shrugged.

She wondered if he knew what Kenneth's end game was.

The ghost spoke softly to her again.

"Kenneth is going to head into that office any second. I'm going to tell your husband that I've let you know what's happening."

She'd have given her eyeteeth to understand how Jackson had gotten into the bank, but this wasn't the time to ask.

The ghost slipped away.

Seconds after he did, Billy looked down the hall, frowning as if confused.

And it seemed as if he'd forgotten about Angela.

He turned and took a step toward the office.

Jackson was in that room.

*Seconds, just a few more seconds…*

Angela knew if she was going to act, it was now or never.

# Chapter 4

Waiting was one of the hardest things law enforcement learned to handle.

Jackson knew it was a waiting game—and one he had to win.

He stood in the office, trying to make sounds that would elicit curiosity rather than alarm.

Something that would draw Kenneth, the cold-blooded member of the team, to him.

Knowing that he had to take the man out without making noises that would create greater alarm and cause a troubled young man in a terrible mental state to start shooting randomly.

But David was there, helping them and keeping communication going between him and Angela when it wouldn't have been possible any other way.

Waiting…

Making the little ticking noise, stopping it, starting it again.

And then…

Jackson was flattened against the inside wall when Kenneth finally stepped into the room.

He moved in a flash, crooking his arm around the man's neck and stopping his ability to cry out, squeezing hard enough to make him lose his breath, tightly enough to keep him from fighting, thrashing, and making noise.

He eased off the choke hold when the man passed out, lest he inadvertently kill him.

Even as the man slipped to the floor, Jackson kicked his gun far from his hand, rolled him over, and then cuffed him.

To his great relief, he immediately heard a commotion in the hallway outside the door.

With Kenneth on the floor, handcuffed and unarmed, he dared to step out, his heart beating just a little quickly.

Angela.

But he needn't have feared.

Billy Mendelson was on the floor with Angela perched over him, wielding his gun. She looked at Jackson.

"Had to borrow his. I mean, we were out with the kids for the day. I wasn't armed. I guess that was good. I don't think they ever knew I was law enforcement."

He smiled at her.

While Kenneth might have been a cold-blooded killer…

Billy Mendelson, not so much. And Angela had known that. She had also known that someone in such a condition could fire out of fear or because he was surprised.

But now…

Billy Mendelson lay on the floor, sobbing.

"I didn't want to. I never wanted to!" he cried.

Jackson barely heard him. His temptation was to run to his partner, his wife, and hold her, simply thanking God that she was all right.

In the professional world, temptation had to be fought.

He pulled out his phone and called Bruce McFadden, alerting him that the perpetrators were down.

"Get them. I'm going for the hostages," Angela called.

Jackson nodded, dragging Billy around to put him with Kenneth, both securely cuffed, while he headed to the front of the bank to open the door and let the feds and local police who had gathered in. When he finished, he discovered that Angela was standing by the vault, trying to communicate with those inside.

"They use an eye scanner. And Elise is locked in the vault with the others." Angela groaned. "There has to be a way—"

"There is," Bruce McFadden announced, coming in with a man of about fifty, professionally dressed, white-haired, looking serious and concerned. He headed straight to the vault and entered the numbers. Stepping forward more, he let the vault scan his eye.

"Peter Grafton, manager," Bruce explained to Angela.

"Thank God," she murmured, stepping back.

Hysterical people began to emerge from the vault. For a moment, Jackson thought Angela's greatest danger might be getting trampled.

The men, women, and children in the vault rushed her, wanting to thank her for all she had done—talking and giving herself to the robbers so they could be safe.

Naturally, there was chaos after such an event. There would be reports and investigations, and it would be a long time before they could just go home and be with their kids.

Paperwork, like waiting, was long, painful, and necessary.

Bruce paused at Jackson's side, speaking quickly. "I took the liberty of calling Mary so she can go and get your kids from the fundraiser. I hope that's all right."

"That was brilliant. I don't know what we—or the Krewe—would do without you," Jackson assured him. "Thank you."

"Of course."

Bruce and his brothers were special agents with their

unit. The Krewe had grown to encompass many agents in every state, and even the Blackbird Division, working in Europe. Thankfully, they were left alone for the most part.

They had an amazing success rate, mostly because they didn't stop. But then again, they had help. From those such as Captain David Clancy.

Bruce—and the other Krewe members who had stepped in to take witness statements—made sure the people in the vault knew they could receive help if they needed therapy, suffered nightmares, or any other such thing. Bruce nodded imperceptibly in David's direction, knowing he deserved their thanks.

Jackson wanted to know him, needed to know a great deal more about him.

It wasn't until the initial melee of the takedown and the following confusion that he remembered what he had seen in the tunnel.

It was easy enough to explain that he'd read somewhere about the tunnel that led from northern Virginia to DC during the Civil War, but damned if he could remember where he'd read about it. Desperation had helped him find it.

The ghost of Captain Clancy watched him with amusement when Jackson explained how he'd gotten into the bank unseen and without setting off any alarms.

Bank robbery was a federal crime, which meant that Billy Mendelson and Kenneth would be taken to a federal facility, one he and Angela had easy access to.

They learned early that Kenneth was Kenneth Martin, an escaped convict who had previously robbed a savings and loan, killed a teller, and was sentenced to life. Of course, a life sentence didn't mean anything if a man managed to escape.

Billy Mendelson was another matter entirely. From the time they took him into custody, he'd begged to talk to Angela.

"I do need to talk to him," she told Jackson, looking at him with a pained expression. "I think Kenneth somehow forced Billy into what he was doing, Jackson. I don't know how, but… Billy is no killer. I played it as carefully as I could because I didn't want him to start firing in panic or because he was startled or…you know what I mean. But something there isn't right."

Jackson nodded. "I remember the case. His house was robbed, and his parents were killed."

"If you've been through that—"

"Angela, people react differently to that kind of tragedy and trauma. Maybe Billy wanted other people to hurt the way he was hurting," Jackson said.

She shook her head. "You weren't with him, Jackson. I'm telling you, something was going on there. And he's in such a fragile state."

"All right," he told her, smiling. "One of the things I love about you, Angela, is that despite everything we've seen and done throughout the years, you still have tremendous empathy. If you're right…"

His voice trailed off. He suddenly thought about the strange bit of white he'd seen in the dim glow of his phone's light in the tunnel.

"What?"

"Um, yeah. You want to talk to Billy. We'll set it up for the morning. As for me… I think I saw something strange in the tunnels. I want to go back down there."

Angela arched a brow and grinned slightly. "You mean you saw something besides fetid water, feces, and that kind of thing? Oh, my God. You do stink. You need a shower—maybe two or three."

"Aw. And all I wanted to do was hold you."

She slid into his arms. "Even stinking like a sewer, you're the best man I've ever known," she assured him. "And there you go. Now, we both need showers."

Night had fallen, and they had finally finished all the reporting, paperwork, and signing they had to do.

Angela would speak with Billy Mendelson in the morning.

And maybe Jackson would get Bruce or another of the McFadden brothers down to the tunnels with him. And David.

The ghost had hung around as they finished up their day. But when they were leaving, he caught up with them outside. Angela, being Angela, immediately said, "I can't tell you how grateful I am, Captain. You saved us all."

David nodded. "My pleasure, ma'am. I can't tell you how it thrills my soul to know that I was able to be of assistance."

"You are such an incredible man," Angela told him. "I'm hoping—"

"I'll come see you, I promise. But I know you have children. You two go on home now. I can't smell anymore, but I can only imagine you stink something awful."

"Okay, okay," Jackson said, laughing. "I smell. I'll go do something about it. But—"

"I will see you at your Krewe headquarters," David promised.

"Thank you," Angela whispered.

David left, and they traveled home.

Corby was a teenager and had heard about everything that had happened. He didn't seem to care that his parents smelled; he was just happy to hug them both. Victoria was younger but sensed how bad things had been and hugged them fiercely, as well.

Even Mary pulled them in, with Angela apologizing profusely as she did, warning her that she would end up smelling, too.

Mary, Special Agent Axel Tiger's aunt, had been a godsend. She loved living near her nephew and looking after Corby and Victoria.

But it was late. When she left, they got the children to bed.

Then they looked at each other and headed for the shower.

"I think I'm too yucky for this to actually be romantic in any way," Jackson told Angela.

She laughed. "I did say you needed several showers."

"You know, some people think it's fun to get down and dirty," he teased, drawing her into his arms as the water sluiced over them.

"I…hmm, I don't know. I don't think they mean *this* kind of dirty," Angela informed him, laughing.

"So, we must get undirtied to get dirty?"

"Something like that."

And so they scrubbed. But scrubbing to get clean was a pretty cool thing to be doing, one that touched all the senses as soap and water slid over them, both together and apart. By the time they no longer smelled of anything but soap, they were laughing and in each other's arms, trying not to slip as they exited the shower and headed toward their bed.

Jackson knew he'd led a hell of a life. But Angela had always been the most amazing part of it. They could almost think as one and made the best partners in the world when it came to work. And when they came home…

They always understood each other. How touching, holding, and being together as one created the beauty in life when it was so necessary, sending their senses soaring. And then later, still lying together, entwined…

But morning always came.

Though waking up beside her was just as beautiful.

When the day began again, they got the kids ready and headed into work.

Once there, Angela left almost immediately.

She wanted to understand what was going on with Billy Mendelson. Psychiatrists might tell her it was a reaction to what had happened to him.

But Angela wanted more. Much more.

As for Jackson, he headed to Bruce's office. The agent was studying his computer and looking baffled when he walked in.

Bruce looked up when he saw Jackson. "Sorry. I'm just, um, perplexed. It's still bothering me. So, you and Angela took down the guys in the bank. But how were they planning on getting away? There must have been someone else out there. The police checked every parked car, but…I was out there, Jackson. I was out there, and I never saw a getaway car or anyone else ready to help them in their escape."

"I wonder…" Jackson murmured.

"Wonder?" Bruce pressed.

"All right, yesterday. Here's the scenario. They're in the money vault. They're being careful, trying to take small bills and cash that can't be traced. Kenneth watches as Billy and Angela choose the money and pack the cases, and I began making an annoying noise—not an alarming one, just annoying."

"Right."

"So, when Kenneth came into the office, he had his gun out."

"That makes sense."

"Yes, under most circumstances, I guess. But what if he knew?"

"Knew what?"

"What if he knew about the tunnels that were part of the sewer system? What if he came into the room, ready to shoot anyone who had also figured out the tunnels?"

"You think he sees the dead, too?" Bruce asked.

"No, no. There are records somewhere. Lost in history, perhaps, but they must have existed."

"You think maybe he was planning to escape through the tunnels?" Bruce asked.

"I'm thinking it's a possibility," Jackson said. "I'm telling you. Naturally, I was in a hurry yesterday—lives depended on us stopping Billy and Kenneth—but something was bothering me."

"What did the captain tell you?"

Jackson shook his head. "I don't think he'd been in there, at least not for a long, long time. We're lucky he knew the old tunnels had become part of the sewer system and that the bank building was there through it all, even if it did serve as something else once. But..."

"Something bugged you, and we go on gut instinct. Your gut says we need to check out the tunnels," Bruce said.

Jackson shrugged. "Yeah."

"Yeah? Yuck," Bruce said, grinning.

"It might be a little better today," Jackson told him. "I called and asked about getting some of those coveralls the sewer workers use. But..."

"Yeah, yeah," Bruce told him. "I've followed you into worse places. So?"

"Into the sewers we go," Jackson said cheerfully.

———·•••·———

Angela was glad for her position with the Krewe as she visited Billy at the holding facility. She was able to assure the guards that she'd be fine with him uncuffed.

She wanted Billy comfortable and at ease as they spoke.

"You," he said as they brought her in. He looked away.

"Yep. Me. Billy, I didn't mean to hurt you yesterday when I catapulted myself on top of you. I think you'll understand I had to get the gun away from you."

He nodded, still looking away.

"Please, Billy. Talk to me."

"Hey. You caught me. But you couldn't catch the bastards who killed my parents."

"I'm so sorry. We weren't on that case, but I promise you now that I'll do everything in my power to see if we *can* become involved."

"They wore masks and gloves," he said. "They even laughed when they talked about it. They weren't going to leave any DNA. No fingerprints." He paused for a minute, his face wrinkling in a mask of pain. "They planned on killing them all along."

"I am so sorry, Billy. So, so sorry. But I know Kenneth forced you into participating in his planned holdup yesterday. What I don't understand is how he managed to do it."

"Does it matter? I'll go to jail regardless. And I don't care."

"No, Billy, you need to care. You're a good person, and I'm going to prove it."

"How do you know I'm so good?" he demanded, looking at her at last.

"Because I'm alive," she told him softly.

That was when he began to cry.

# Chapter 5

"Really?" Bruce said, tromping through three feet of waste. "Wow. Okay, I have faith in you, oh, great leader."

Jackson groaned. "Come on, Bruce. Look, I'm sorry—"

He cut himself off as he reached the area he'd been in the night before.

"Joking, mostly. You don't need to be sorry. I always thought the Underground Railroad consisted of routes and safe houses to get those in slavery to places where it had already been abolished. I didn't know—"

"Ah, yes, my friend. You're right," David said. "That was the Underground Railroad. And, yes, it was established with all kinds of routes and houses—and some of those routes had to do with old tunnels, as well. Some natural caverns in the earth could be expanded and used even today for all kinds of reasons. When I was a little kid, if we got as far north as DC, some amazing abolitionists were incredibly good and brave human beings, ready to help us on the rest of our journeys. And President Abraham Lincoln signed the Emancipation Proclamation, of course, so the world began its trek to be a little bit better for all human beings in the country. It was a long road, one it seems we're *still* on, but I always have hope that we'll eventually see the value of every living person, regardless of color, sex, and so on. But for today, I'm here to help."

Jackson pointed at the shimmer of white he'd seen when trying to reach the bank the other day.

"I need to see what that is," he told David and Bruce.

"Let's do it," David said, leading the way.

But he stopped suddenly, standing dead still.

Staring.

Jackson moved up next to him and saw what the ghost had seen, what his phone's light had picked up last night. Bone.

There was a skeleton stuffed into the wall.

"I…don't think it's a recent murder," David said.

"Maybe not a murder at all. Perhaps someone just got…stuck in here," Bruce wondered aloud.

But Jackson shook his head. "I believe Kenneth knew about the tunnels and intended to use them when he finished robbing the bank. With his background, I'm afraid that…"

"You're afraid the bones may have been here for a long time, and there might be more," David assumed.

"Did you see something else?" Bruce pressed.

Jackson made a face, looking from the man to the ghost. "Gut feeling," he said simply. "All right, I know I dragged you into a sewer—"

"Jackson, just ribbing you, I don't care," Bruce assured him.

"It obviously means nothing to me," David said. "Can't smell anything anyway. Not that you dragged me in here at all."

"So, we have a skeleton. We're going to need to get forensics and a medical examiner down here."

"We'll get our people. Kat Sokoloff is an ME," Jackson said. "This place needs to be thoroughly investigated."

"Sewer workers come down here," Bruce said thoughtfully, looking at Jackson. "But probably not into the walls like the little holes you crawled through. As far as they know, those places just need work."

Jackson was already heading toward the skeleton.

The remains were not entirely down to the bone, but it appeared as if they had been there for a very long time. To know *how* long, someone educated in forensic pathology would need to consider the dampness, the temperature, and more.

Scraps of clothing adhered to the bone, but nothing that could tell them immediately about the era in which they might have been worn.

"This is…an ungodly mess," Bruce said, shaking his head. He looked at the ghost of Captain David Clancy. "Did you—?"

"Did I know about this?" David asked. "No. I think you were saying something about it earlier to Jackson. The Underground Railroad really referred to safe houses and trails that people could take to get to safety. Like these, there were tunnels in certain places, hideouts in the Blueridge Mountains and elsewhere. But I don't think I ever heard of anyone dying down here. Plus, the tunnels were used during the Civil War. They were a great way to get injured men off the field and to help."

Bruce looked at the man, nodding his admiration. "You saw a lot of action," he said softly.

David nodded. "But even in battle, I never got used to killing others. Even someone who thought so little of a man like me. It's not natural for human beings to kill other human beings. At least, not in my mind. I guess even cavemen went after each other, but I like to believe that human decency is still stronger than any hate group, bringing it back to something as tragic as the Civil War or up to some of the things that happen to this day. Then," he added with a sigh and a pained expression, "you get the truly sick individuals who can attract their own kind—a man or woman without a shred of common human decency or empathy."

"I think we may be dealing with something like that here," Jackson said. "But Kenneth was in prison until he escaped just a few months ago. So—"

"So, he's been working with someone," Bruce said.

"And they know about the tunnels," Jackson added.

"But," the captain said, "they don't know about me."

"True. Our secret weapon," Jackson acknowledged, nodding.

"Split up now? Take different areas?" Bruce suggested.

"That's a plan," Jackson agreed. "If you want—"

"I'll head south," Bruce said and shrugged. "Smells just as bad everywhere."

"Again, it makes no difference to me," the ghost told him.

Jackson smiled.

Being around a ghost with a great sense of humor was kind of fun.

———————••••———————

"I think... I'm not sure..."

Billy Mendelson began to talk, then stopped, shaking his head.

"Billy, please. I swear I'll help you," Angela told the young man. "You think something has to do with Kenneth, right?"

He nodded slowly, wincing.

"Billy, was he one of the men who broke into your house?" she asked.

"No. I mean, I don't think so. But..."

It was like pulling teeth, but Angela knew she had to be patient. He was terrified again, and he had been traumatized. She tried to remember every second of what had happened in the bank.

When it began, Billy had been the one to speak. But Kenneth had been down on the floor in front, acting as if he was just another customer.

But he was armed, and he knew how to use a gun.

He certainly watched every move Billy made.

"All right. Kenneth wasn't one of the two who broke into your home, but he knows who they are. He knows them, is friends with them, is working with them, something," she said.

He threaded his fingers through his hair, leaning on the table, tears streaking down his face again.

"Yes, he knows them. Or maybe you're right, and he was one of them. He—he found me after the funeral," Billy told her.

"But—"

"He put the gun to my head and fired it, just missing me."

"He threatened you. He made you do what you did."

Billy nodded.

"Billy, if he threatened your life—"

"Not my life," Billy protested. "My life now…it's worthless, it's just a cycle of pain."

"Billy, you can get over that. Counseling will help you. Do it for your parents. You have so much promise—"

"No matter how you spin it, I tried to rob a bank and threatened other peoples' lives."

"You never meant it, and you never killed anyone. Billy, please, trust me. I don't have all the answers, but I believe in an afterlife. I know your parents would want you to go on and become the brilliant man everything up to this point has led you to," Angela told him passionately.

He almost smiled. "You're a beautiful person, you know that? I don't mean just the brilliance in your eyes or all that golden hair. You're really beautiful inside, where it matters," he said. "I knew that yesterday. I knew you wanted to live, but you would have died before letting anyone else take a bullet."

"As you might have figured out—"

"You're a cop."

"An agent. And you have every right to want to know who killed your parents. We'll take it to my unit now, and I promise we will not stop, Billy. You went along with Kenneth, which tells me you want to live, too."

He started to laugh.

"Billy—"

"I told you. I don't give a damn about my life."

"Then—"

"You don't understand. He has Cassie."

"What? Who is Cassie?"

Tears suddenly ran down Billy's cheeks again.

"He never should have gotten her. I mean, after it happened, with my parents. When the police came, and I went to the station…they sent me to a hotel for a few days because my house was a crime scene. I was so upset that I called Cassie and…she was supposed to be at camp with a summer college prep group, but the trip was still in the DC area. She came to see me. But when she left my room, she never made it back to her group. She called them to say she was following up on some research, but… I know what happened to her. I know what happened because Kenneth told me. He swore they were holding her. He even put her on video for a minute. They made her call her parents with a ridiculous lie so she wouldn't be reported as missing. But the thing is, we're both eighteen, so we're adults and…"

He broke off, sobbing.

Angela set an arm on his shoulders, trying to calm him.

"Billy, we're going to do everything in our power to find Cassie. But I need to know absolutely everything you know about what happened and where she might be. Please, Billy. I need you to calm down."

"They shoot people and think nothing of it," Billy protested. "The bank job went bad. She's probably already…"

She wouldn't let him say the word *dead*.

"And she may be alive. Help me, Billy. Please, I'm begging you. They'll keep her alive if they think she can be useful in any way. Please, please help me so I can help you. If there's any chance at all, we'll find Cassie."

He tried to gain control of himself. "They kept putting her on the phone with me—"

"They?"

"Kenneth. He told me if I did everything he ordered me to do, she'd be okay. He would see to it that they let her go. But then the bank heist went to hell and…well, I'm being held in jail, awaiting arraignment, and they're going to kill her."

"Give me a second," she told him. "I'll be right back."

She left him and put a call through to Jackson, quickly telling him everything she'd learned.

"We can put a trace on Billy's phone—"

"You know they're calling from a burner," she interrupted.

"But we can get some traces going, see what we can learn and…"

"And?"

He took a breath, likely knowing she wouldn't want to hear what he was about to say.

"Angela, we found a skeleton—"

"A skeleton? It couldn't be Billy's friend Cassie so

quickly," she told him.

"No, it isn't Cassie. They're sending people to get the bodies out of the tunnel."

"Bodies?!" She tried not to scream the word but…

"Three of them, I'm afraid, including the skeleton. Angela, I believe Kenneth knew about the tunnels, too. Figure he was going to use them for his escape route. The skeleton may be decades old, but another victim appears to have been there for at least a year. One man couldn't have been dead for more than a week. We're still…"

"Looking. I'm going to tell Billy goodbye and be on my way," she told him.

"Angela."

"Yeah?"

"We still need to talk to Kenneth. He may give us something. Maybe—"

"You're right. Except with a man like Kenneth… I don't think he'll give us anything at all. And, Jackson, he's going to be arraigned. There isn't enough bail money in the world to let him out. He must have been working with someone, someone who is holding on to Cassie now."

"And that could be anywhere," Jackson said. "Angela—"

"I'll try. I'll try, and then…"

"I want this kept with the Krewe for now. The captain is proving to be an invaluable asset, and I want to keep it that way. But we have plenty of agents in the city right now, and I have Kat coming to autopsy the bodies. Get what you can—"

"I will. And then I'll be down there with you,"

They ended the call, and Angela winced. She had to go in and speak with Billy. He needed one of the best defense attorneys they could find.

Returning to the interrogation room, Angela tried to offer Billy an encouraging smile. "We're going to get to the bottom of this, I promise you. Let's start with Cassie. I need her full name, Billy."

"Cassandra Marie Payton. She's eighteen, beautiful, sweet, and good—all the best things a person can be. You have to find her."

"We'll do our best. Everything we can," Angela promised him. As she spoke, she texted headquarters. They had one of the best tech squads possible, and she knew that because she worked with them all the time.

By the time she left Billy, they'd have pictures and every bit of information possible on the young woman. They'd have scoured her social media.

They'd know what they were looking for and more.

They'd know if Billy and his parents had been set up or if anyone had stalked or harassed them or Cassie.

With all the assurances Angela could give him, she left Billy and spoke to the guards.

In a matter of minutes, she walked into another interrogation room and faced Kenneth.

A man who looked amused to see her.

One who appeared completely confident—despite the fact that he was to go on trial for armed robbery.

"Ah, if it isn't the sweet little thing who twisted that fool boy around her pinkie," Kenneth said. "If only that meant it was all over," he added.

She hadn't asked for his restraints to be taken off. In fact, he was cuffed, and his cuffs were attached to a bar on the table between them.

She smiled. "Actually, I'm fairly tall for a woman. And as you've discovered, I'm not a sweet little thing at all but a federal agent," she said with a shrug.

"And there you are, exuding confidence. But guess what?" he said, leaning toward her. "You're going to need to start a whole lot of negotiating here if you want my help—and you are going to need it."

"Oh, I'm not so sure. I mean, you're facing federal charges. We're opening a new investigation into the events at the Mendelson home, so you'll be charged with murder, armed robbery...so many charges. If you get helpful, well, we are looking at federal charges. With everything you've done, it might be in your best interests to do everything you can to get the death penalty off the table," Angela told him.

He started to laugh again. "You're going to scare me with the death penalty?"

"If anyone dies over state lines...it's a federal case. And you know—"

"The death penalty takes forever."

"Sometimes."

"You're a proponent?" he asked.

"Not particularly," Angela said with a shrug. "But my feelings don't really matter. What matters is the law. And we're talking about a human life right now."

Kenneth shook his head.

"You know, I don't get it. You're a good-looking man and not so old yet that you couldn't serve your time and have something of a decent life. So—"

He groaned. "Don't you get it yet? That little bastard caused the entire thing. I didn't break into the Mendelson home. I didn't kill anybody. That snot-nosed kid threatened to kill me if I didn't help him rob the bank. I mean, talk about being traumatized and messed up. Lady, you should know by now that trials aren't always as cut and dried as you think. I mean, you've only gotten one side of the story. That kid is messed up. Such a momma's boy."

"You're the one with the record."

"Yeah?"

"Escaped convict," Angela reminded him.

"Okay, well, you try being in prison. The kid somehow knew it. That's why he came after me. I was easy prey for him. Now, if you're really a decent human being, you'll care about the girl he's kidnapped and turned into a hostage."

"Okay, let me understand this. Billy Mendelson was a straight-A student with an incredible life ahead of him. His parents were brutally murdered—probably by you—"

"Oh, hell no. Don't go blaming that on me."

"Back up. Think about it and tell me. Who should I believe? A great kid or an escaped con. Who would you believe?" Angela demanded.

"That's the point. You're not seeing the whole picture, or only seeing what you want to see. Billy. He's weird but smart. So smart. A straight-A student. And after what happened? The poor boy is dealing with so much. But don't you see? That's just it. Horrible things happened to him, played with his psyche, and put him in agony. Then he turned that agony into something awful, trying to make other people suffer in the same way he did."

"I don't know. In the bank, I was much more afraid that you'd go off than he'd just start shooting," Angela said.

Kenneth groaned. "Mark my words. He's got a girl out there somewhere. And I can almost promise you, while you idiots are falling for his stories, that girl is going to die."

# Chapter 6

Had people been using the sewer tunnels for body dumps? Was it a secret passed down for years through criminal enterprises?

Jackson stood looking at the fourth corpse they'd discovered since he'd followed his instincts to search for the flash of white he'd seen when Captain Clancy had shown him the way to the bank.

He wished he had more medical experience. The body was clearly that of a man, and Jackson thought he had been of medium height and build in life, maybe five-ten and a hundred and eighty pounds.

His clothing had mostly disintegrated in the tunnels' fetid conditions.

His face had disintegrated, too

He lay on a strange shelf that nature had created underground. And while the space didn't appear to have been dug out, it still had the look of something that might be found in the catacombs in Rome.

He felt the captain come up behind him.

"I had no idea," David said softly.

Jackson shook his head. "We're going to need a forensics

team down here, and it's beginning to look like a slew of medical examiners, too."

"Another body," David murmured.

"I'm praying there's still a chance of finding Cassie alive," Jackson said.

"There's still more down here that the sewer workers don't get to. Come on, I'll take you down another corridor. At least, I assume it still exists. I mean…I knew this all existed because of the past. But I realize I'm a ghost. I understand that I'm dead, though I'm not sure…well, I've seen others leave. Sorry. I mean, the point is, not even ghosts like to hang around in the sewers. There's a sports bar a couple of blocks down from the bank, and I take pleasure in watching all the games they show."

Jackson managed to smile. "Good to hear you're enjoying your afterlife—and not hanging out in the sewers," he told him.

His phone rang. Angela.

He answered it quickly.

"Hey, anything?"

"Yep, a bigger tangle than ever before. I mean, the obvious would be that Kenneth is a true criminal—a killer, robber—devoid of anything resembling empathy. A psychiatrist would need to judge the man. But he claims Billy Mendelson was destroyed by what happened to him and finds solace in making sure everyone around him suffers just as much. Kenneth claims we're all ignoring the obvious, and says Billy is the one who masterminded everything that went on at the bank. He also said that Billy is the only one who can tell us where to find the girl."

"You believed him?" Jackson asked doubtfully.

"I don't want to, that's for sure," Angela said. "Anyway, I tried. I tried and tried. I'm on my way down there. At this point, I'll be more useful searching for the girl than trying to get one of them to break."

"They are both still being held? And neither has asked for an attorney?"

"Not yet. And they're holding off on the arraignment, trying to determine just who they're charging with *what.*"

"You don't think—?"

"Jackson, I'm so frustrated. I feel like I need to be moving in a different direction."

"Of course. If we don't find the young woman soon, I'll take a stab at the two of them. Come on down. It's, uh, great down here."

It was getting better. Several members of their forensics teams had arrived and were working in the areas where they had found the bodies.

Still...

"Come on. Follow me. I'll lead you astray," David promised.

Jackson groaned. "Great. I'm searching a sewer littered with the dead with a ghost who has a weird sense of humor."

David laughed at that. "Sometimes," he said softly, "you need to go with the humor, you know? I remember the war, seeing friends..."

The ghost's words drifted into silence.

"I'm so sorry," Jackson said softly. "I've served, so—"

"So, you know," David said. "On the positive side, we won the war in the end. Decades and decades later, people began to realize that we're all human. But then, you're... Indigenous, right?"

Jackson laughed. "Yep. Kind of a mutt. Dad's family is Native American. Cheyenne. Thus, the surname: Crow. Anyway—"

"Ah," David interrupted. "And the criminals you take down have to eat crow."

"Ha, ha."

"Hey, I like it. But in the world, the struggle for us to accept and care for one another no matter our heritage, leanings, whatever, will always be ongoing," David said. "But I like to believe in humanity. Think there are far more decent human beings than…well, okay, so even though we're looking through ancient tunnels connected to a sewer for bodies and a kidnapped girl, I still believe in the decency of most human beings."

"Great. So, let's find that girl alive."

———————••••———————

"Is it possible?" Angela asked Jackson, shaking her head. "We know Kenneth Martin is a criminal, a horrible person, one who has committed crimes in the past and shouldn't be believed. But what if he happens to be right? Can it be true? I spent time with Billy in that bank. I watched the two of them. But…"

She paused, shaking her head.

"But?" Jackson pushed softly.

"When they first came in, Kenneth was down on the floor. Billy was waving the gun around—pointing it right at one of the kids. And when a security guard moved, he swore he'd shoot, and both the guards turned everything over. Billy is the one who demanded that the bank customers put their cell phones in a bag they passed around. And it wasn't until it was all underway that he pointed out Kenneth."

"And Kenneth…"

"Was on the floor with everyone else," Angela said.

"That's not a bad plan for a bank robbery—having a hidden asset in case things start to go wrong," Jackson reminded her.

She saw Jackson smile suddenly. They were deep into one of the side offshoots of the strange piece of the tunnel that had brought them to the bank.

She turned to see that their ghost friend had come upon them.

"Hello!" he said softly to her.

"Hi, David. Thank you so much. You're still helping us, I see."

"I wish I was more useful," he told her.

"David, you might have saved over two dozen lives yesterday. I call that amazing help," Angela assured him. "I don't know what you heard…"

"Well, here's the thing. There's the known criminal, and there's a young man who suffered unimaginable pain and trauma. It's not impossible."

"But it is improbable," Angela said, shaking her head. "Neither is talking, so…"

"Hey!" Jackson said. "Bruce was going into holding. David, maybe he can give you a lift, and you can, you know, quietly hang around both and see if they talk to themselves or there's anything you can determine."

David grinned at that. "I can try to give them a few chills," he said, then shrugged, looking perplexed. "It's amazing…being dead and being here. It's so incredible to find not just one but several people who see and hear me. And who knows? I think I mentioned this to Jackson, but I keep thinking this whole thing could be why I'm still here. So I can give you more of a happy ending. I guess in your line of work…well, you know—on finding this young woman, anyway."

"Let's go find Bruce," Jackson said.

"I'll keep heading down this way," Angela told him.

"And I'll be right back," Jackson promised.

Jackson departed with the ghost, and Angela took a moment to look around her. She'd never expected such a maze of underground tunnels—albeit part of the system that was now the area's sewers—in this area where northern Virginia met up with Washington, DC.

She imagined that years and years ago when David Clancy was a child, there had probably been a natural formation of caverns or the like, though they were far from the mountains. She tried to remember her geography. DC was on land ceded by Virginia and Maryland. The Anacostia and the smaller Rock Creek fed the Potomac River, and the capital sat in the flood plain of the rivers, surrounded by high ridges and terraces.

Maybe the tunnels made sense, though she wondered if they flooded during the rainy season.

In days gone by, did criminals count on the flooding to hide any vestiges of their crimes?

Such as the bodies of the deceased.

She gave herself a mental shake. She was looking for a girl who might still be alive—no, who *was* alive. She had to be. Cassie.

"Cassie."

She said the name aloud and then decided that speaking out loud and calling as she moved through the tunnels might not be a bad thing.

She began to move, and as she did, she noted another of the dark crevices to her right. She shone her phone's light on it and saw that it had a narrow slit.

Narrow but enough for a body to slip through if one went at it horizontally.

"Cassie?"

She moved to the narrow opening and realized she could slip through it—and so could someone even larger than her if they managed the right angle.

But could they have forced someone else through it?

People could be very obedient when someone had a gun pointed at them.

Unfortunately, she'd need to do it almost entirely in the dark because she couldn't keep her hands on her phone while attempting the maneuver.

Phone pocketed, she worried that her small work bag, Glock, and holster might hold her back.

But she wasn't letting them go. And it was only a matter of maneuvering all her body parts the right way.

She gripped the lower portion of the ragged earth and stone and very carefully worked to lift her body into the right position to wiggle through it. For a moment, she feared she was slipping. Then she discovered she was lying flat—or almost—in the crack in the wall. With just a little maneuvering, she found herself on the other side.

She heard whimpering then, not quite a cry but a sound someone might make if…

If they had cried and shouted themselves out.

"Cassie! Cassie, are you in here?"

There was silence for a second.

Maybe she was afraid of who might be coming for her.

"Cassie, my name is Angela Hawkins Crow. I'm a special agent with the FBI. I swear to you, I'm here to help."

"Please, no. Don't kill me! I haven't done anything, I swear, I…"

"It's okay. I'm not going to hurt you. I'll get you to a hospital, and we'll find your family. Cassie, it's going to be okay."

Angela heard a cry again and trained her light down the new tunnel where she stood. At first, she didn't see anything.

Then, where the wall narrowed, and the ceiling seemed about ready to fall, she saw a figure huddled in a corner. She hurried to cover the distance, kneeling beside the young woman.

She was filthy, of course, covered in the dirt and grit of the caves. Her hair was a long tangle around her face.

And she was bound. Her wrists were tightly tied together, as were her ankles.

Angela was glad she hadn't discarded her work bag. She always carried a small pair of scissors—something she had learned throughout the years.

The ropes were rough, and it took her several tries to saw through them, but she eventually freed the young woman from the ties.

"You're Cassie, right?" Angela asked her softly.

"You didn't come to…to…"

"Cassie, we've been looking for you," Angela said.

"To make sure I was dead?" the young woman whispered.

"No, no. To get you out of here," Angela assured her.

She heard a muffled shout from the other side of the strange, horizontal opening.

"Angela!"

"No, no, no!" the girl cried.

"It's okay, it's really okay. That's Jackson Crow. He's going to get us out of here. They'll break up that part of the wall so we don't have to slither through it again," Angela assured her. "It's okay, Cassie. It's really okay. I swear we're here to help you."

She left Cassie for a minute to hurry to the hole, shouting back to Jackson.

"How the hell did you get in there?" he asked her.

"A lot of twisting and turning," she called back. "Jackson, we need some equipment. Cassie is here, but she's not in great shape. I don't think it would be right to try to wedge her back through. Can we get some equipment—?"

"On it. Two minutes," Jackson told her.

And he was right. He returned by the time she'd reached Cassie's side to keep her reassured.

The forensic teams were in the tunnels, and they came

with equipment, though she really hadn't expected anything heavy…like whatever Jackson was wielding to knock down the wall around her horizontal hole.

Cassie sat shaking as Angela gently held her.

The wall burst open with a scattering of dirt, concrete, and stone.

Cassie screamed, but Angela tightened her hold on the girl and assured her everything would be okay.

Jackson stepped into the clearing he had created as Angela urged Cassie to stand.

She did but instantly swayed.

If she'd been here for days, she had to be seriously dehydrated.

She started to fall, but Jackson hurried forward and caught her, lifting her into his arms. Cassie's face bore a look of panic.

Angela took her hand and assured her they were going to the hospital, saying she would be all right.

"But the monster will find me, he will come for me!" Cassie cried.

Angela stared at her, frowning.

Jackson was quick to tell her, "No, no, Cassie. We're not going to let any monsters get to you, I promise. There will be officers and agents with you at the hospital, and I promise you, we will not let any monsters get to you."

The girl just kept sobbing, but Jackson was getting good at navigating the tunnels and sewer. Angela moved fast to keep up with him.

Soon, they saw daylight up ahead and an ambulance waiting.

"I'm going with her," Angela told Jackson.

"We're both going," he said. "We'll get scrubs there. They aren't going to want us in a hospital, and I don't blame them. We can tag team showers."

Jackson had a way with people. The paramedics had no problem with them entering the ambulance; they were already tense over the situation and determined to stop anyone involved in whatever was going on.

As a young paramedic started a saline IV for Cassie, Angela gently asked her what she meant. "Was the monster a man you're calling a monster?"

"No. A real monster," Cassie told her.

"Can you tell me what it looked like?" Angela asked.

"Blue…blue fur, strange face, maybe like a gorilla, but it spoke English and had a knife, a gun, and…and another monster. Both blue, both furry, with those faces…I don't know. I mean, I don't want to insult gorillas—gorillas aren't monsters; they're just animals. But these…they were real monsters. They caught me in the dark as I was headed to the subway, and…one put a gun to my head. The other held a knife to my throat, so I just did what they told me. I did everything they told me!"

"They made you slide through the wall?"

"One went first—to show me. To wait for me. To tie me up so I couldn't move."

They arrived at the hospital. Doctors moved quickly to assess the damage that hunger and dehydration might have done to the girl.

Jackson and Angela took turns standing in the hall. One of them stood watching over the girl while the doctor in charge arranged for showers and scrubs they could wear until other agents and local police officers could relieve them.

Monster.

No. Monster*s*.

Cassie was terrified that they might be coming after her again.

The doctor had explained to them that Cassie was lucky to be alive. They had found her just hours before dehydration might have taken her life. She was receiving treatment and sedated so she could calm down enough to heal and not panic and rip at the IV sending fluid back into her body at a proper rate.

She might be more rational by morning. That would be the time to talk to the girl.

Axel Tiger took over for them, along with Will Chan.

While Jackson believed that whoever had done this in costume wouldn't head into the hospital with a blue fur suit and a gorilla mask, there was always the danger that someone might make an appearance pretending to be hospital staff.

Therefore, they'd be watching over Cassie.

And they needed to let her family know what had happened.

Angela would assume that task.

"And," Jackson said, "I'm going to take another run at our good friend Billy Mendelson. We need to know if he's truly a victim coerced into doing what he did, threatened with not just his life but also that of a friend. Or is he a victim so traumatized that he turned into a monster?"

"Well, here's one thing," Angela told him.

"What's that?"

"No matter how good a costume, he couldn't possibly be *two* monsters," she said dryly. "We need to find out if it was Billy *and* Kenneth, or if it was Billy *or* Kenneth with an accomplice on the outside."

# Chapter 7

Jackson headed back to the police station to speak with Billy Mendelson.

The ghost of Captain David Clancy had told him he'd planned to hang around the men in their separate cells, hopeful one of them might mutter the truth while sitting around.

If a ghost could look weary, that one did.

Clancy was seated at the foot of Billy Mendelson's bunk, his head in his hands. He looked up when he heard the guard coming to escort Billy into an interrogation room to speak with Jackson.

Jackson gave David a barely perceptible nod. In turn, Clancy just shook his head. He hadn't heard anything.

Billy looked at Jackson eagerly when he was seated across the table from him, the guard having left to close the door and leave the two of them alone.

Of course, it wasn't really just the two of them.

The captain's spirit was with them, as well.

"I can see the question in your eyes, Billy, and I'm going to waylay your fear straight away. We found your friend, Cassie. She was hidden in those tunnels."

"You found her?" Billy said.

"Yes, we found her. She might have died soon of dehydration, but we found her in time. The doctors say she's going to be all right."

"Oh, my God, thank God. Thank God," Billy breathed. "Did she tell you what happened?" he asked anxiously. "I have to see her. I need to tell her I'm so sorry. I know they went after her because of me. She's so sweet and wonderful. I'm so grateful, so very grateful."

"You can't see her right now, Billy."

"Why?" He lowered his head. "I told you I never wanted to rob the bank. I never wanted to do anything bad. I did what Kenneth told me to do so he wouldn't hurt Cassie. And you found her alive. He hadn't killed her—"

"Billy, I'm sorry. We're still talking to the assistant United States Attorney—federal crime, bank robbery—"

"No! You're feds. That's why you're trying to turn this into more than—"

"More than armed bank robbery, Billy?" Jackson interrupted. "I'm sorry. I'm truly sorry."

"I never touched Cassie. I swear. I was willing to do just about anything to save her life!" Billy protested. "Cassie will tell you—"

"I'm afraid Cassie believes she was kidnapped by monsters. Of course, she likely means people dressed up as monsters," Jackson told him.

Billy was silent, his head hanging.

"But she didn't recognize either of them?" Billy asked, shaking his head.

Was that relief on Billy's face? Had he been one of the kidnappers?

Billy looked up at Jackson, tears in his eyes. "There were two. Just like at my house. Just like when my parents were murdered. Two of them. At our place, they didn't dress up as monsters; they just wore masks so they wouldn't be recognized."

"All right—"

"If they hadn't given up on finding my parents' killers, none of this would have happened. Not the bank, not Cassie, not…" His voice trailed off, and he sobbed.

Jackson believed the man's emotions were real.

But it still didn't tell him if Billy might have been involved in what had happened at the bank—or what had been done to Cassie.

Maybe trauma had turned him.

Perhaps it was a way to make law enforcement pay more attention to the fact that his parents had been murdered.

"Billy—"

"Kenneth. He's a monster with or without a costume," Billy cried.

"Well, according to his past record, he *is* a monster. However, whether he's one of these monsters or not remains to be seen," Jackson reminded him.

"Don't you have forensics? Gloves, costumes that cover the hands, whatever. There must be something. Haven't forensics gotten incredibly advanced? Like, you didn't find a hair, a fiber, anything yet?" Billy demanded.

"Nothing that proves anything. Whoever snatched Cassie up did so weeks ago. When did you find out there were old tunnels that branched off the sewer system?" Jackson asked.

Billy frowned. "Um, well, I've never been in them. Kenneth said they were there and told me he'd find a way into them when it was time to leave the bank. He knew all about them, I guess, though I don't know…well, I mean, I don't know how he meant to get into them or where they let out. I just knew he had Cassie, and if I didn't obey him, he'd kill her."

"How was he planning to kill her when he was with you in the bank?" Jackson asked.

Billy frowned as if he'd never pondered the question.

"I just… I mean, I knew he'd gotten her and had her… somewhere. I didn't know anything about the tunnels until that day. And then I thought he might have buried her somewhere. If I shot and killed him, I'd never know where she was. Maybe he had someone working with him outside the bank. If he did, that person would likely kill her if they didn't get their part of the loot," Billy said.

It sounded true.

Plausible.

Jackson nodded. "Well, you can rest assured in this: Cassie is okay. I'll speak with you again later."

"Wait! Am I being arrested?"

"You've already been arrested. And read your rights. You chose to speak with us, though you can call for an attorney anytime."

"But…what am I being charged with?" Billy demanded.

"At the moment? Armed robbery. Billy, Kenneth is claiming it's all your fault. Right now, the attorney has determined that you both must be charged."

"But I didn't want to do it!"

"I'm sorry. The charges may be dropped if we can make a few more discoveries that help you," Jackson reassured.

"Kenneth is a monster. He has to go back to prison no matter what, right?"

"Correct. But he'll have a few more charges added to those he's already been convicted of."

Billy closed his eyes tightly.

"I didn't…I…well, I did do it. And I guess I'm willing to pay. If Cassie is all right, then whatever happens is worth it."

"Billy, trust me, we're all hoping the best for you. What you went through was horrible."

"And you'll try to find out who robbed my house and killed my parents, right? You're not lying? The cops…they said they tried. They said they didn't have any evidence. And I couldn't give them a decent description of the people who broke in."

Jackson nodded. "Trust me, Billy. I know they wanted to find the killers. Tell me. What *do* you remember about them?"

"Average," Billy said wearily. "Medium height, medium build. Faces masked."

"Scars on their wrists or anything like that?"

"I couldn't see their wrists. They wore sweatshirts and gloves, and the sleeves on the shirts covered their wrists. I couldn't see anything about them at all," Billy said with frustration.

"Men who weren't very big. Kenneth isn't very big, but…"

Exactly when had the man escaped from prison? He remembered what they had learned about Kenneth Martin. He had been given a life sentence already for robbing a savings and loan and killing a teller.

And he'd escaped with plenty of time to take part in the robbery at Billy's home. He'd had an accomplice then.

He probably had an accomplice now. Someone out there had been planning to be in the tunnels, ready to bring Kenneth and Billy out of the bank in an escape route through the system.

While escaping, the two had probably planned to tie Billy up in the tunnels, as well, leaving him to die where no one would ever find him.

Unless…

Jackson gave himself a mental shake. Kenneth had been convicted of armed robbery and murder.

It was truly doubtful the man would tell the truth.

Jackson glanced at the ghost and gave him a brief nod. Billy didn't notice.

He was staring at the table.

He looked up at Jackson. "Will you tell her, please? Tell Cassie how grateful I am that she's going to be okay."

"I will. For now. We'll try to arrange for you to see her."

Billy looked at him with tremendous hope in his eyes. He smiled and nodded at the guard, rising. Billy did the same.

When the man had escorted Billy away, Jackson spoke to the guard again.

"I'd like to see Kenneth Martin again for a few minutes."

"Want him chained to the table?" the guard asked. "They want him back where he's supposed to be, you know. Not sure a trial will matter with him. He's already doing life."

"He needs life without parole," Jackson said.

The guard shook his head. "He got out of federal prison without parole. Guys like him…do you know how he got out?"

"No, I don't. But he's been out long enough to have been involved in the murders of Mr. and Mrs. Mendelson, right?"

"Yeah, we were all warned. He faked a heart attack. Escaped from the infirmary and made it to a laundry room— and then out with a truckful of sheets. The guy is always maneuvering something."

"Not a good guy. Be careful."

"Oh, I guarantee it. He'll come to you in cuffs."

Jackson nodded.

Cuffed yet grinning, Kenneth took a seat at the table in the interrogation room again.

"You still don't get it, right?"

"I still don't get what?" Jackson asked him.

"You know. Think about it. No one ever found anything. And yes, cops can be extremely incompetent, trust me. But I think in the case of the Mendelson couple, they tried pretty hard. No one saw the supposed killers. No one saw any kind of a getaway vehicle. Don't you think it's possible that Billy killed his own parents? Maybe they beat him or did something to ensure he was such a brilliant, straight-A student. Maybe he just couldn't take it anymore."

Jackson groaned.

"Couldn't describe anyone, right?" Kenneth asked, sitting back and smirking. "I mean, think about it. Seriously. What difference does any of this make to me? I go back to life in prison no matter what. Why would I make this up?"

"Let's see. Because you'd enjoy it tremendously if we wound up believing you and prosecuting Billy for the murder of his parents as well as being the brains behind the bank robbery," Jackson said dryly.

"Why would he be so willing?" Kenneth asked.

"Could be you told him you'd murder his friend if he didn't," Jackson said.

"What friend?"

"Cassie—Cassandra Payton," Jackson said. "We checked. She wasn't with her camp group or her parents. Someone used her to threaten him."

"I don't know anything about any girl," Kenneth said.

"Right."

"I don't. Not really. But think about it. If she was his friend, he probably took her. And she's probably dead already."

"Sorry. She's been found."

"Alive?"

"Alive."

"Well, that's great. Ah, then maybe she'll tell you herself that Billy is the guilty one."

"Yeah, maybe. Or perhaps she'll describe you to a T," Jackson said, watching the man. Kenneth just shrugged and shook his head. He wasn't worried about anything that Cassie might have said.

And why would anyone be worried about anything

Cassie said since she'd been kidnapped by monsters?

Costuming. He had a feeling Kenneth was good at it.

And he wasn't getting anything else here. It was time to head back to the hospital and see how Cassie was doing before checking in with Bruce and the others to find out what, if anything, forensics and the medical examiners had discovered about the tunnels.

Bodies. Left through the ages. It was horrible to accept, even if they were to discover the victims had been killed decades ago.

As Jackson headed out of the building, he smiled.

The ghost of Captain Clancy had fallen right into step with him.

"You can't let it drive you too crazy," David said.

Jackson turned to him and arched a brow.

"What you're discovering in the tunnels," David said. "The skeleton. Maybe it's been there more than a hundred years. The others…they weren't your failures. And you found the girl before she—you found her alive. You need to be grateful for that."

Jackson smiled at the ghost.

"I am. And we're grateful to you. She wouldn't be alive without you."

"No, being dead doesn't mean you know everything," David assured him. "At least not while…while a man is still hanging around on Earth."

"Well, we are grateful that you hung around."

"Team effort," David said, then shrugged, grimacing. "Life was hard but beautiful. I remember the safe houses—and these tunnels—when my mom took us away from our owner. You know, I don't think he ever came after us. We were just part of the economy. He wasn't a cruel man, but…well, I don't care what continent you're on, no human should ever own another."

"Agreed!" Jackson told him. "But it does still go on. Not legally in most cases, but the world is full—"

"Of those who will use others…yeah. I do what I can when I can."

"I'm sure you do. Escaping, the war, everything after—it must have been hard."

"I got a good job after the war. I'm exceptionally good with horses and worked for a great fellow who raised them. I married and saw my children grow up, as well as my grandchildren and great-grandchildren. One day, I know I will join those I loved who went before me. But until we discover just who was doing what with that whole bank thing…well, curiosity has always been a thing with me, alive or dead."

"Great. Let's see what kind of a read you get off Cassandra Payton. She should be feeling a little better by now."

"Monsters," David said and shook his head. "There is someone else out there. Someone who was in on that heist. Someone who was, perhaps, supposed to make sure the girl Cassie was dead once the heist had been completed."

Jackson nodded. "Somehow, we must discover who."

Jackson's phone vibrated in his pocket. It was Angela. He answered it quickly.

"Hey. Anything?"

"Cassie was out for a while. Her parents are here with her now. I told her you'll want to talk with her a bit when you get here, but…all I'm getting—still—is a tale about monsters. Oh! The hotel the cops put Billy up in while his home was closed with crime scene tape happens to be about a block away from an entrance to the sewers, oddly enough. If Billy wasn't in on this and had nothing to do with Cassie's kidnapping, whoever did most likely saw her leaving Billy's hotel."

"That was weeks ago. She'd have been dead if she was in

the tunnels for that long, starving, and with no water."

"But she might have had someone taking care of her at first. When you get here, we'll try to talk to her again."

"And her family seems to be okay? They never knew she had gone missing?" Jackson asked.

"She was supposed to be having a wonderful time on a camp outing, but they filed a report the day before the bank robbery. That's when they figured she'd been busy and having fun but really owed them a call."

"Remind me to talk to our kids every single day—even when they're supposedly grown up," Jackson said.

"Well, kids can get involved with friends, jobs, camp."

"Right. I'm on my way in."

"Great. Is David with you?"

"He is."

"Wonderful."

"Monsters," Jackson said wearily. "She can only tell us that she was kidnapped by monsters."

"Come on, Jackson," Angela said. "We've been in law enforcement for a long time. And we've always known that human beings are capable of being the worst monsters out there."

"Right. And you are right. I shouldn't need to be reminded."

*Monsters, indeed.* He glanced at David.

He knew the ghost was just as eager as they were to find the monsters who had kidnapped and nearly killed Cassie and threatened the lives of so many.

Jackson was certain, in one way or another, that the murders of Billy's parents were just the beginning of a much larger plot.

# Chapter 8

"I—I don't know how long I was there," Cassie told Angela. "The monsters came at first. They brought me food and water—not often, but enough. But when they were bringing me through…"

She broke off, wincing.

"What is it, Cassie?" Angela asked gently. "We need to catch those monsters, stop them, and we really need to understand who it might have been and if there were several of them, just two, or—"

"Two took me the first night," Cassie said. "And then… one was smaller than the other. The one who forced me through the wall was the one who brought food and water most of the time. If there were more than two of them…I'm so sorry. I don't know. I was mostly in the dark, the pitch-black . I think I…passed out a lot. I even thought I had died a few times. But then I heard you. Still…"

Her voice trailed off again.

"Cassie, I know how hard this must be for you. And I'm so, so sorry. I will leave you alone, and you can be with your parents in just a few minutes, I promise," Angela told her. "And…I honestly believe if you talk about it all, it may get a little better. It will get better every day now that you're out of there and can heal. So, if there is something else, please tell me."

"They showed me corpses first," Cassie said. "Before they tied me up, they showed me people…rotting. They warned me that if I didn't obey them, I would become one of the dead. And, toward the end…they just didn't come anymore. I knew then that they'd always wanted me to become one of the corpses."

Tears dripped off Cassie's chin.

Angela got her a tissue and said, "Cassie, we found you, and you're not going to become one of those corpses. You're a survivor, young lady. You've done beautifully and beat them."

Cassie looked at her hopefully and smiled through her tears. "I did survive," she said. "I survived monsters!"

Angela nodded her encouragement and stood. "I'm going to get your mom and dad. I think they're going to release you from the hospital today. You'll get to go home."

Cassie nodded, looked at Angela, and whispered, "Thank you."

"Thank you for being so strong," Angela told her.

"I don't know. I may be afraid to go out for a long, long time. Then again, well, maybe I'll take a self-defense class and make sure I don't wind up in any dark alleys by myself again."

"Good thinking," Angela advised her. But that, of course, led her to another line of possible questioning.

"You went to see Billy Mendelson that day?" Angela said.

"Yes. Poor Billy. He was in such bad shape, so devastated. Not to mention depressed and desperate. He said they'd never get the people who had done it because he wasn't able to help them. I mean, Billy wasn't attacked by monsters, but he was confused by what he saw because he didn't know anything about the people who broke into his home. He couldn't see their hair or skin. He couldn't tell if they were young or old, if they had tattoos—or anything at all that might identify them. They were long gone, even though he'd dialed 911 hysterically the minute they were gone. He wished they had killed him, too, rather than leaving him with his parents shot and nothing—nothing at all—he could do for them. I tried to help him. I tried to tell him he had to move forward in their memory. Said they would want him to live life to the fullest and be happy. They had been happy. He had given them happiness, being such a great kid and student."

"Cassie, you mean everything to him," Angela said.

Cassie winced. "I heard them talking, saying Billy was part of a bank holdup—the holdup that, thank God, sent you into the tunnels and made it possible for you to find me. But Billy…he didn't turn bad. He couldn't have been one of the monsters because there was no way he could have gotten ahead of me."

"That's good to know," Angela told her.

She smiled.

Billy may not have been one of the *monsters*, but he might still have been part of the plan. Had he known that Cassie would be taken?

She didn't want to believe that. And Kenneth Martin had a criminal record. Of course, any lead or suggestion needed to be checked out.

But having listened to Billy and now Cassie…

Angela thought the two cared for each other. They were good friends, even though it didn't seem that they had been a couple. Friends could care very deeply, and it was possible for a high school boy and girl to be just really good friends. Angela had had several male friends herself in high school with no romantic attachments.

But…

How had Kenneth convinced Billy that he had Cassie? He hadn't called Mr. or Mrs. Payton—she'd asked them that when she first met the couple.

"Cassie, it's truly a pleasure to know you. You are an incredibly strong young woman, and I know you are going to do well in life. Take care. I'll see you again."

Angela headed out.

"Thank you," Cassie called after her.

Cassie's parents were waiting in the hallway, looking at Angela anxiously. She still wasn't sure how the girl had been gone so long without being reported as missing, but maybe she was being judgmental. Cassie was a good student, and from all she had learned, she was a good person who was now legally a loved and trusted adult. Her camp had been all about learning, and it might have been a show of faith that her parents trusted her to enjoy herself without calling home every other minute.

And the camp?

Well, sometimes, and for various reasons, people just didn't follow through with plans they made.

The director had told her that all campers had been required to check in by a certain date and that it had been in the *large* print that those who failed to show voluntarily gave up their positions unless they provided a doctor's note.

Never. Never, never, never would she let it happen to her children.

For a moment, she wondered if she and Jackson might not wind up being overprotective because of what they did for a living.

Of course, they were different to begin with.

Angela assured Mr. and Mrs. Payton that Cassie was doing fine and that they were doing everything possible with all manner of local and federal employees to get to the bottom of what had happened.

Jackson was due at the hospital anytime now. Then they were to meet with Bruce and the others at headquarters to find out what might have been discovered forensically.

To find out what, if anything, might be discovered about the four bodies they had unearthed in the tunnels.

She should just head in, but…

She pulled out her phone and called Jackson.

"Anything?" she asked him.

"Kenneth accused Billy, Billy accused Kenneth. Same old, same old."

"Well, one new bit. At the very least, Billy was not one of the so-called monsters that kidnapped Callie. She's certain he wouldn't have had the time to get into that kind of a costume and get down to the alley to grab her as the monsters did."

"Good to know. I'll take a turn at the hospital. Then we'll meet back up at headquarters. Are you—?"

"There are still sewer and forensics crews working the tunnels. I'm not sure what it is, Jackson, but something is calling me back there."

"Gut," Jackson said.

"It could be crazy, but…"

"Yeah. Gotcha. Okay, I'll see you at the office in a few hours."

"See you there."

"Angela?"

"Yeah?"

"Be careful."

"You know me. I'm always careful."

They ended the call, and Angela headed for her car. It was a short trip to the entrance, which was now permanently open.

She spoke to the sewer workers, thanking the man who gave her coveralls.

She would still need one hell of a shower when she left, but the coveralls were great.

Once underground, Angela headed through the strange labyrinth—now widened—to find the tunnel where she'd slipped through to find Cassie huddled in the far rear corner.

Now, of course, the wall had been smashed.

But she could still imagine it as it had been the day before. Narrow. She closed her eyes and thought about the place in absolute darkness.

It was, in fact, amazing that the white light of a phone's flash could provide such illumination in such a stygian place.

But…

Okay. Obviously, someone had known about the tunnels. It did seem most likely that it was the escaped convict, Kenneth Martin.

Then again, Billy had been a stellar student.

Maybe one of history and geography. Somewhere, there had to be a written record mentioning the tunnels being here as part of the Underground Railroad that had even preceded the Civil War.

She had brought her tablet, but it was unlikely she'd get Wi-Fi where she was. Maybe her phone was working.

She put a call through to the office. In a few minutes, she was speaking with Whitney Tremont, an agent who went way back with her—to their first case as the Krewe of Hunters in New Orleans. Not that they didn't trust all their agents and find them to be the best—and most *talented* or *cursed*—in the field, but Angela had known Whitney and worked with her forever. So, it was easy for Angela to explain to Whitney what she wanted and why.

"I really believe it's ridiculous that a kid might have manipulated a master criminal, but…see what you can find in records, books, podcasts—anything—that mentions these tunnels. If we can't find anything, then Billy Mendelson couldn't have found anything either."

"We do have both Billy and Kenneth in custody. And you found the poor girl who was kidnapped," Whitney reminded her.

"But someone else is involved, and we can't solve this thing until we find out who," Angela told her.

"All right, I understand that," Whitney said. "I'm on it. I'm not as good as you—"

Angela broke in with a laugh. "You might be better."

Whitney laughed softly, too. "I will do my level best."

"There's more, of course. I promised I'd work on finding out what happened to Billy Mendelson's parents. The law can't give up on him."

"Angela, you're the next step to the boss—the supervisory special agent is your husband. But while we promise to do our best; we don't promise to achieve," Whitney reminded her.

"I know. But, Whitney, I know it's all connected. Somehow. We need to find that connection."

"Okay. I'm headed in for my history lesson now. I'll get back to you asap."

"Thank you."

Angela studied the stone, closing her eyes for a minute to remember what it had looked like and recall the horizontal slit that had been there before Jackson blew a hole in the wall.

Only one of the *monsters* had come in to see Cassie with food and water. That would have probably been the smaller of the two.

Despite Jackson's size—a man who stood well over six feet tall and kept fit as their lives demanded of him—he would have gotten through if he had to. But…

It was so much easier for a smaller person.

They kept thinking men were the culprits here. *A smaller person.*

What if the unknown person was female? It was more than possible. While most serial killers proved to be men, it was not impossible for a woman to slide into the role.

And while this wasn't such a situation…

It didn't mean a woman wasn't involved.

"Special Agent Hawkins."

She turned to see one of the forensic team, a young woman named Belle Mabry, standing back.

"Hey, Belle."

"I just wanted to let you know we've been all over in there, collecting bits of food the rats hadn't gotten to yet, trying to see if there are any prints, hairs, or anything else anywhere."

"Great. Thank you. Anything?"

"A few hairs, believe it or not, caught in the ragged parts of the stone in the wall. They're being tested now. Of course, they may all belong to the young woman who was kept hostage down here, but…"

"Anything is worth a try," Angela assured her.

"I'm off. I just wanted to let you know."

"Thank you. Oh, hey, what color was the hair?" Angela asked.

"Reddish, maybe auburn."

"Thank you."

Belle waved a hand and disappeared.

Cassie's hair—once it had been washed—was dark blond, almost light brown. Billy had dark brown hair and Kenneth was blond, as well.

Of course…

Those hairs could have been stuck on the tunnel wall forever.

Hair lasted longer than flesh and human organs. She pictured the skeletal remains they'd first recovered.

Angela's phone vibrated, and she answered it quickly.

"Anything?" Angela asked.

"Something, maybe. I'm not so sure I like history. I've been reading about the Massachusetts 54th during the Civil War. My God. After the first two years, Abraham Lincoln knew he had to make use of African troops. And the Emancipation Proclamation only freed slaves in the states that were in the rebellion—I mean, I guess the North was filled with abolitionists at the time, but soldiers joined that unit from as far away as Canada and the Caribbean islands. Anyway, sorry. Your new friend, Captain David Clancy, was with the Massachusetts and is incredibly lucky he survived. Six hundred men were sent in to attack Fort Wagner, protecting Charleston, and more than half of them were killed. But those who survived went on, and thankfully, David was among them. He wound up befriending a fellow who worked for a DC paper at the time. There was even an article where he talked about coming to freedom through the tunnels and how he would have given his life, if necessary, to achieve it. It's a great article. But the point is, if I found it, others could have, too. And that means they at least heard of the tunnels."

"Thank you, thank you, Whitney. So…I am almost positive it was someone else, our missing third person, who knew about the tunnels, and might be a redhead," Angela told her.

She frowned suddenly, remembering the bank.

And while it seemed impossible and preposterous…

She suddenly realized she might know who the third person was. And while it did indeed seem impossible and preposterous, in a way…

It made sense.

"Help! Help me!"

Angela spun around, the soft cry from beyond the area where she stood looking at the broken wall catching her attention. The sound came from where she had found Cassie Payton huddled on the ground the day before.

Angela hurried around the broken wall, anxious.

*What now?*

And then she knew. She knew because the second she came around the corner, she felt the steel against her skull.

Déjà vu.

Then came the warning, a harsh whisper.

"Don't move, or I swear you're dead."

# Chapter 9

They often took turns questioning people. Sometimes, one agent might have a question that jarred something in a suspect or witness. Other times, they just might have the right empathy to draw out more.

But Jackson quickly discovered at the hospital that there was little more—if anything—he could gain from Cassie.

And she was happy, even seeming to be healing from her ordeal. She was so relieved to be with her parents.

She was calm and ready to talk.

She just didn't have anything more to tell him, though she was willing to go through the whole thing again, going to see Billy...

And heading into the alley. Night. Darkness.

And monsters.

And she believed in her friendship.

She told him she was anxious to see Billy.

"I know he was forced to take part in that holdup. And I believe with my whole heart that they forced Billy by telling him they'd kill me. I really want to see Billy."

Jackson glanced at her parents.

They looked at each other and then at Jackson, both

nodding solemnly.

They trusted their daughter.

"All right," Jackson said. "But first, Cassie, what's most important is that you make sure you're doing well after everything you have been through, and the doctors say it's okay. When that happens, I'll make sure you see Billy."

"Thank you," Cassie told him.

He hesitated for just a minute. "Cassie, you're sure—absolutely sure—that Billy couldn't have been one of the monsters who kidnapped you?"

"Oh, I'm positive. I left his hotel room and went out the hotel's back entrance. I never should have done that, but it made it a closer walk to the subway. But the thing is, I was barely in the alley before they grabbed me. There's no way, seriously, no way at all that Billy could have been one of them."

"And you believe in him," Jackson said softly.

"With my whole heart."

"And you don't think he would have been traumatized into violence?"

"No. No, the only thing Billy wanted was for a police officer to speak to him in a way that was positive. They kept telling him they had nothing. And I think they made him feel that it was his fault because he couldn't describe the men. He couldn't tell them anything at all."

"The police didn't tell him they wouldn't investigate, did they?" Jackson demanded.

"No. He said he believed they were trying to be kind, bracing him for the fact that the killers might never be found. And that bothered Billy."

"Enough to make him lose it and want to hurt someone?"

"Billy?" Cassie said. "No, no, no. No way. He wanted the killers caught because he never wanted anyone to feel as bad as he did."

"Thank you, Cassie," Jackson told her.

He smiled and managed to leave, pausing to exchange a few words with the local officers before he left, and one of his agents from the Krewe of Hunters: Bruce's brother, Brian McFadden. He didn't think anyone was coming after Cassie where she lay in the hospital.

But they could never be sure.

There was still an unknown entity out there. Someone who had been involved in all of this—perhaps even the murders of Billy's parents. And while there was no longer a chance to reap the rewards of a bank robbery, the killer certainly did not want to be identified.

And thus, guards were always on duty.

When Jackson arrived at headquarters, Bruce was waiting.

"We have an ID on one corpse. The man was Walter Raintree. He disappeared in the nineteen seventies. Foul play was suspected. He was a witness against the mob boss, Henry Marino, and the case fell apart when he didn't show up for court. Since his body was never found…well, it's a little late now. Marino died seven years ago. Kat and several other MEs examined all the bodies, and one seems to have been there for almost two hundred years based on carbon dating. Another body they estimate to have been there since the nineteen twenties, and the last corpse is from nineteen eighty. They're still trying every DNA database in the world for an ID, but since the fingertips were chewed off, there's no chance of finding an ID through prints."

Jackson sighed. "Probably not much chance of us getting justice for any of these people at this time. Still, if we can solve this…"

"Billy's parents."

"Yeah."

"Well, I hate to say it, but Kenneth has been going on and on about the kid doing it himself. No getaway car spotted, Billy can't identify anyone…"

"How does Kenneth know all this?"

Bruce arched a brow. "You know as well as I do that the murders were plastered all over the news channels, the Internet, and what remains of our newspapers."

"Right. Of course. So, have you seen Angela yet?"

"She hasn't come in," Bruce told him. "Whitney talked to her when she was in the tunnels. She wanted her to get on the computer."

"I knew she was going to the tunnels." He frowned worriedly. "Something was drawing her back. You know how it is when you think you almost know something and returning to a scene might be the impetus to discovering what it is."

"Jackson."

He and Bruce turned.

Whitney Tremont came hurrying over. "Jackson, she's still at the tunnels. She asked me to do some research to find out if information about the old tunnels was online anywhere. I found something written about Captain Clancy several years after the Civil War. She needed to know just who might have found out about the tunnels. But, Jackson, I just tried to call her again. I know she's down in those tunnels. I tried to tell myself there might not be any service down there, but we've gotten through before. I—"

"Headed to the tunnels," Jackson said.

"We're coming, too," Bruce told him.

"The more the merrier."

Angela was smart and capable. She had probably been the one influence that had kept everyone alive during the botched bank robbery.

But she was in ancient, fetid tunnels and might have

figured out who the unknown accomplice was…

Just in time to meet them in the flesh.

———————...■■■.———————

An old saying swept through Angela's mind.

*Still waters run deep…*

And there was more that they or the local police should have done regarding the bank robbery and what happened.

They had known who was guilty, so…

*Why look a gift horse in the mouth?*

She actually managed to smile, furious with herself and ready to mock because she should have known. She had known, or, at the very least, she had come to suspect the truth—just a few minutes too late.

"Bingo! I mean bingo. Yes, I am a woman, and not a big one. I'm not a woman like you—oh, so tough. Trained to stay calm and cast herself down like a sacrificial lamb whenever there's trouble. No, that's not me. But you see, when I'm holding this great invention of man—the gun—in my hand, I'm just as tough as any piece of flesh out there."

"That is true, Ms. Benton," Angela said. "And, yes, you can shoot me. But I am curious. No one had any idea—"

"No one had any idea?" Elise said. "Well, that idiot was going to give me away eventually. Do you think they actually teach history anymore? I was amazed to discover that I had an absolutely perfect escape from the bank. And that's just it. Once I get you out of the picture—"

Angela didn't try to turn.

Elise Benton was not an experienced or hardened criminal. But…

She might have been the mastermind behind the bank job. And…

Was it possible? Had this assumably vetted and respectable assistant bank manager been one of the masked pair who had killed Billy Mendelson's parents?

"Right now, I am all powerful," the woman crowed.

"That you are. And you are so right. I've discovered that through the years," Angela told her. "I mean, you know who I am. So, wow, yes. I've been up against some big bruisers. You know men always think they're more powerful than women, and…"

"We know better. This really is a shame. I like you," Elise told her.

"You're pretty amazing, too. I mean, the way you managed everything at the bank, Elise…well, if you hadn't been working with idiots, you'd have gotten the money and made your way through the tunnels."

"Go figure on that, will you? These tunnels have been here forever. And no one—not even the idiot sewer workers—knew they existed. It's really not my fault. Seriously. Think about it. What do they teach in schools these days? How to sign on to your favorite video game? History, geography…people know nothing. So, it seemed the right thing to do. I mean, after…well, like I said, you know a woman can be as powerful as any brute. All you need to do is put a gun in her hand."

"I'm here. And I'm going for help."

Angela almost smiled. The ghost of Captain David Clancy was in front of her, assuring her that she had help.

But could help come fast enough? And even if it did…

Cornered, Elise would still have the nose of her gun pressed to Angela's head. And she might be willing to die herself when someone else entered the picture—someone with a gun trained on her.

For a moment, Angela clearly saw David in front of her.

And she thought Elise shivered slightly as if a cold draft had come into the room.

Elise wasn't one of their strangely gifted or cursed numbers; she couldn't actually see or speak to the dead.

But she could sense something when the dead were near. She could sense something cold that elicited shivers within her.

*Might that help at some point?*

But then David was gone, and Angela knew he was going for help. He had seen the entire situation. She believed he would explain it well and make it possible for others to do whatever they could.

Without putting her into greater danger.

 She wondered if he knew he'd given Elise shivers.

But he'd have realized that just giving someone the chills might not be enough. He had gone because he believed the best thing he could do was get to Jackson or someone else who could help as quickly as possible.

Under these circumstances, she needed to figure out a way to help herself. Certainly, she was far better trained when it came to anything that resembled a physical confrontation, but there was little opportunity for that when all Elise had to do was twitch to pull the trigger.

"Elise, you are ever so right. You are the total power now. But I wish I could understand what led to this. I mean, this all has to be new. You must have been vetted to get your position at the bank, and you are the one who helped save people… So, I mean, I wish I could understand how you became involved with Kenneth or Billy or…I just don't get it. And…" She let out a sigh. "I know. I mean, I think sometimes we're not at all appreciated. I—"

"I had the experience. I had the seniority," Elise snapped.

"At the bank?"

"Twenty years of my life. I was young. I had a chance at a life, love, a family. But no. I was always the one who worked overtime and went in when there was a problem. And yes, I got promotions. But…"

She was upset, and the gun was still pressed against Angela's head.

"Oh, my God. You're kidding me. You put in all the work. You put in overtime. You made the bank everything in your life and those bastards promoted Peter Grafton over you. And you knew. You knew Grafton would call in with some excuse—he was supposedly the manager, but he always had an excuse. A meeting with the main bosses for the bank chain. Something with his wife or one of his kids. You knew you'd be the one in the bank that day, and you could huddle whoever was there into the vault and behave like a brave savior to see that people lived. And you knew the bank robbers would get all the money they needed."

Elise laughed softly. "But you were there. And you really were willing to throw yourself under the bus. It was all going so well. But you made me look even better."

"Oh, Elise, you are so clever. They were incredibly stupid not to see you were the right one to be the manager. There's just one more thing I can't figure out."

"Really? And you are oh so clever yourself."

"Well, better than a lot of those bruisers out there, but not nearly as clever as you are, Elise."

"Right. Because you think you're manipulating me right now."

"I'm not, Elise. I know the power of a gun. But I'm seriously lost. I just don't understand. Please, before…well, please, grant me one favor. Let me know how you got started on this whole thing. Did you know Kenneth, Billy, or the Mendelson family? Please explain how this all came about, I'm begging you. I'll get on my knees."

"You'll get on your knees—for me?"

"Yes. You said you liked me. Please, grant me that small

mercy. Let me understand how this all happened."

The nose of the gun shifted around Angela's head.

"Down. Down on your knees," Elise said.

Angela carefully obeyed, noting Elise's height, her hand on the gun, and where they were in the tunnel.

At some point…

She had to decide. Take a chance, judge her moment, duck, and lunge for the gun.

It would be her only chance.

"So, please, please tell me. Did you meet Kenneth somehow, or Billy? How did this whole thing come about?"

"Well, you see," Elise explained, "in another life, I might have been a great actor."

"Ah. I get it. You were one of the monsters," Angela exclaimed. "Oh, Elise, you must have been amazing."

"I was kind of amazing," Elise said.

"And…wow. So, who has been telling the truth? Kenneth claims it was all Billy—they must have met after Kenneth escaped from prison. But did Billy hate his parents? Did he kill them? Oh, wait. The Mendelson family banked with you. That's how you knew them. And with your position at the bank, you knew where to get the cash that couldn't be traced easily and…"

"Fine. I'll tell you all of it. You can take it with you to the grave."

# Chapter 10

"She knew. She knew!" the ghost of Captain David Clancy told Jackson. "The red hair. As soon as Angela heard a red hair had been discovered, she knew who the third person was."

"Elise? Elise Benton?" Jackson said, still furious with himself. Why hadn't any of them seen it? Suspected? Why hadn't they determined right away that someone in the bank might have been involved?

Especially Elise Benton, whose office had the entry to the tunnel.

He could argue with himself that there had been no reason to suspect that anyone in the bank had been involved.

They had caught Kenneth and Billy in the act.

That didn't matter now. Because he knew Elise Benton had a gun to Angela's forehead.

They were in the car, getting to the tunnel entrance as quickly as possible. Bruce sat next to Jackson.

David Clancy was in the back seat.

"Should you have gotten a slew of agents or officers out?" David asked. "I mean, I guess it's just one woman—"

"Exactly, David, but one woman who has a gun pressed to my wife's head. And you said Angela had her talking, right?”

“Right. From what I heard, I guess Elise Benton just cracked. She gave her whole life to that bank, and then they promoted Peter Grafton over her. The final straw in her mind? She believes they promoted a man over her, even though she had better qualifications and greater seniority.”

“She might have been right on that. But it seems she managed to snap with a plan in mind,” Bruce commented.

“Angela has her talking,” Jackson said, then glanced at Bruce, who nodded.

“If we go in and accost her,” Bruce explained to David, “she could decide she’s finished and might as well take Angela with her.”

“But…Angela needs help.”

“And we intend to help her. Geography won’t be a great help,” Jackson said dryly. “What we’ll do is try to get into positions where”—he glanced at Bruce again—“we can take action if we need to. We’ll have to find positions where we have clear shots—shots that can take her out instantly. But you don’t know Angela. She’s pretty amazing. She may be able to talk Elise down to a point where she can end this without any more death.”

In the rearview mirror, Jackson saw the captain’s ghost looking perplexed.

“Maybe she should die,” he said softly.

“We aren’t judges or a jury,” Jackson said quietly. “But—”

“You’d let Angela die?” David demanded.

“No. But I also know her, David. She’s my wife, the mother of our kids, and she’s been my partner in all this since we began. I know her. And to save her, we’re going to make sure we’re silent, in position, and—”

“I can help,” David said.

“You’ve been helping us every step of the way,” Jackson assured him.

"No. I mean, I may be able to distract the woman," David said. "She shivered."

"She sensed you?" Jackson asked.

"Yes. So, maybe…"

"Let's get there and pray that Angela is as good as we think she is and has managed to keep Elise talking," Bruce said, then looked at Jackson. "You know, if we weren't the Krewe—"

"I'd be asked to step down because my wife is involved. If we weren't the Krewe, Angela and I couldn't even be in the same unit," Jackson reminded him. He looked at Bruce solemnly. "I'm all right. I can do this. Because we all know what we're doing."

Bruce nodded and smiled.

"Right. And we all love Angela and hate killing—even a killer."

"And maybe, just maybe, Angela is getting the answers we all need. All right. We're there. A few forensic folks are still here, but we're going in as dark as possible. No orange suits. Thankfully, we have a tendency to wear dark suits. Lights kept down."

"And I'll show you the way," David said. "They're behind where you broke the wall to get to Cassie. One of us—well, one of *you*—will need to slither flat at the broken point in absolute silence. That will be the only way to get a gun trained on the woman."

They were at the entrance.

Jackson looked at Bruce.

"Let's do this."

------------

"I knew Billy," Elise said. "Because, of course, his parents did their banking with us."

"So, did you think Billy wanted his parents dead?" Angela asked. "Did you go to him with this idea? How did Kenneth get in on it?"

Elise started to laugh. "You think Billy was the one who provoked the whole thing?"

"I told you, we haven't known what to think. I mean, we figured someone else had to be in on it, but Elise, we had no idea. I mean, no idea in the world that you might have been in on it."

Elise laughed softly again.

But thus far, neither her pleasure in explaining how clever she was, her laughter, nor her reactions had caused her to move the nose of the gun from Angela's head.

"No, no, no. But Kenneth is good, right? Really good. He had you convinced that it might be true. That stellar boy Billy might have been ready to revolt, see his parents dead, quit being such a Goody Two-shoes, and head off to an island filled with beautiful women with a ton of money. He's almost as good an actor as I am. Seriously, I'm not calling you stupid, but it was something you needed to consider."

"So, Billy is entirely innocent."

"Yes, but it will never play out that way."

"How did you meet Kenneth?"

Elise smiled. "Oh, you people. You never knew. Kenneth escaped free and clear, stole clothing off a clothesline, and broke into a house—and I mean to tell you, that man was clever. He watched. Knew how to get clothing without it being noticed and where to slip into a house to steal a bank card without being seen or anyone even knowing he was there. He changed his appearance." She laughed. "He could even steal razors and hair dye without being noticed. And then he came into the bank with that bank card, not expecting to meet anyone more clever than him."

"You."

"Indeed. Despite the disguise, I knew who he was, and it hadn't been that long since I'd been passed over for the promotion. After all the years I put in…well, I managed to get a message to him."

"You wrote him a message?"

"Oh, come on, what do you think I am? Stupid?"

"No. Obviously, you're not," Angela assured her.

Elise nodded. "Obviously," she agreed. "I saw him at the teller's station and walked up as if I were being the ever-charming assistant manager, welcoming him to the branch, suggesting that he might want to speak with me in my office."

"Very clever. So, when you got him into the office, you suggested the bank robbery and told him about the tunnel. Because you knew."

"Of course, I knew the tunnel was there. I read. I went to school. I got a college degree back when they taught something other than how to play video games and get on the dark net to enjoy porn. I read about the tunnels that had existed years ago and knew how to manipulate our cameras and security. I knew the building had changed through the years: it had originally been built back in the 1850s. And I searched. When I discovered there was an entrance from my office, it was like a sign."

"I guess that *would* have been like a sign," Angela said.

"Oh, it was. And with Kenneth in my office, I was so perfect, explaining all the benefits of our bank but managing to arrange a meeting with him far from the bank." She smiled. "We had coffee. He really is a charming man. And so good-looking."

"So, you two hit it off right away," Angela said.

"We did. And when I explained we'd need a second robber so I could appear to be one of the hostages, desperately hoping just to live and save others' lives…well, that's when we came up with the Mendelson family."

"That's why you killed the parents and spared Billy. You needed him off balance, and then…did you get him in on it right away?"

She shrugged. "I didn't do the killing."

*That might be important,* Angela thought.

"Kenneth was good at it, I guess," Angela said.

Elise shrugged. "Well, he could shoot someone without the slightest compunction. Of course, we had to make sure we totally terrified Billy first so he was broken and pliable once his parents were dead."

"But that wasn't enough. Because while Billy might have hated the world, that didn't mean you could totally manipulate him. When cornered, he might have broken. He might have turned you both in. Except…" Angela paused. "Except I don't think Billy ever knew you were involved, did he?" she asked.

Again, Elise chuckled. "I told you. I could have been an actor. He never saw me out of the mask. He never even realized I was a woman and the real power behind everything. But come on. You must get that. You're so good at what you do, but Jackson Crow is the boss."

"You know, Elise, in my case, I love the way we do things. Jackson has his hands full. Between the States and Europe, we have dozens of Krewe agents. And he's not the boss of bosses. There's the fellow who started the whole thing. A man named Adam Harrison. When Jackson is there, he manages the mess of people around the world. When he's gone, I'm in charge. And when *I'm* gone, we have a special agent named Bruce McFadden who holds down the fort. He has two brothers who also take over. We are all good at what we do, but…history. Research. That's my love. That's what I do. And I keep all that running. And as you know better than most people out there now, research—history—is incredibly important. To tell you the truth, in my dreams, the person who gets the job is just the best person for the job, regardless of sex, sexual orientation, color, creed—you name it. Just the right person. Of course, I realize that didn't happen for you, and it was wrong. So very wrong."

"Yes it was. And you see that," Elise told her.

Angela gave her a smile. "Oh, Elise. Billy never knew who you were. So, you watched after everything happened. Watched Billy. You tore apart his home and knew Cassie was a dear friend, someone who really mattered to him. And then you waited, biding your time, watching when he went to that hotel. And you were prepared. So brilliant. You and Kenneth were ready, dressed in your monster costumes. You went after Cassie so you'd have something to hold over Billy. And you kept her alive in the far reaches of the tunnels so you could prove to Billy that you hadn't killed her so he'd know it was up to him to save her life."

"Hell of a plan, wasn't it?"

"Hell of a plan," Angela agreed.

Where the hell did she go from here?

"Did you know about the bodies in the tunnels?"

Elise swore softly. "No. My one mistake. No one knows about these stupid tunnels. It was a perfect plan. And that's why I'm so sorry. You're the only one who would have put a single red hair together with it being me who was the insider on the job. Those other idiots will keep believing—"

"Hey!" Angela said suddenly.

David was back. Which meant Jackson had arrived.

Elise frowned, her hand tightening on the gun.

But she didn't slip.

"Hey, what?" Elise demanded.

"Okay, I'm sure you researched us. The Krewe—"

"Called in for occult and weird cases. Yes, of course. Voodoo, witchcraft, all that—yes, I've researched you."

"Well, we're weirder than that."

"How?"

Angela smiled sweetly. "We don't just handle weird cases. We *are* weird. We can see the dead and talk to them, too. There's a great guy who stayed behind. His name is

Captain David Clancy. He once had to escape slavery through these tunnels. And he became a force in the Civil War. Thankfully, he lived a nice long life after that. But he knew all about the buildings that existed back then, as well as the changes, the sewers…and that they attached to the old tunnels. Anyway, I said, '*Hey*,' because he's back with us now."

Elise was shivering.

"A dead man is with us?" she said, starting to laugh. "You're whacko. It's amazing that you have a job at all."

David was there, and Jackson was there. A tiny glitter of light at the far end of the space let her know that Jackson had somehow slipped in. He was getting a good bead on Elise, ready to shoot if need be.

And if she couldn't distract Elise soon…

"You feel him. You know he's here."

"I don't feel him."

"Yes, you do. You're shivering. Oh, Elise, you're not just brilliant; you're also like us," Angela exclaimed. "You know, I can help you. Forensics has that single strand of red hair, and other people might note you're one of the few redheads who might have been around, but come on. I can help you. Look at you. You *know* the captain is here."

"No. No, that can't be true. It's cold in here. That's all it is."

"I'm telling you the absolute truth. The ghost of Captain David Clancy is here with us."

"Where?" Elise demanded.

Angela was running out of chances. She wanted to live. And if she could keep Elise alive, as well, they had a chance to really give Billy Mendelson the hope he needed to learn to live a new life.

"He's over there, in the corner," Angela told her.

Jackson made a noise, startling Elise and making her turn.

Angela made her move. She grabbed the woman's wrist and aimed the gun toward the back wall.

It went off.

But Angela brought Elise down. Jackson was instantly at her side, kicking Elise's gun far from her grasp and hunching down to read the woman her rights as he handcuffed her.

Angela looked across the room at David Clancy.

"Thank you," she said aloud.

The man nodded, giving her a tremendous smile.

Elise was screaming and protesting, but Bruce McFadden had stepped into the space, as well. He and Jackson were ready to deal with their suspect.

It was over. Really over.

They'd stopped the bank robbery.

They'd gotten all the people who were involved.

And they'd solved the murder of Billy's parents.

Now…

Now, they could finally give Billy some peace and maybe, just maybe, his great friendship with Cassie would lead to more.

Definitely a reason for Billy to live.

# Epilogue

"I was never really in any danger," Angela told Jackson.

He groaned. "Yeah, gun to your head, held by a woman who thought she was overlooked and had already taken part in murder, bank robbery, and kidnapping…"

"Okay, but—"

"You knew you could talk your way out of it."

"You, Bruce, and David did arrive at a really good time," she admitted.

Jackson smiled and put his arms around Angela.

They were in the shower again. There had been paperwork, but Bruce had thankfully taken over with Elise and was finishing up with the attorneys. So, they were able to get home.

And into the shower.

Oh, how she loved showers.

"We're alive. We're here," she whispered.

"And you do feel really good all soapy," he told her.

"Oh? I don't feel good when I'm not soapy?" she demanded.

"No, no. You feel great, absolutely great…soapy or not.

It's just that when you're soapy, my hands slide over you. *All over you…*"

"And mine just slide on everything," she teased.

And proved her point.

Completely scrubbed from all reminders of the sewer, they laughed, managed to leave the shower without falling, played some more with the towels, and then fell into bed together.

It was late—many hours later—as they lay together, her curled in his arms, Jackson staring up at the ceiling, when she murmured, "We need to find David again. He seemed to disappear when we had Elise secured and—"

"We'll find him," Jackson assured her.

"You sound certain."

"I am. I know he isn't here tonight because…" Jackson broke off, smiled, then told her, "Because, thankfully, he led a good life after the war. And he knows what it's like to be in love and be with the one you love after a night like we had."

"Right. He's giving us our privacy."

"But we'll find him in the morning."

"We need to, Jackson. Just think, if it hadn't been for him, things could have gone way differently at the bank. Billy was never a killer, but Kenneth was. Kenneth…"

Jackson made a face. "The man may get the death penalty after this."

"I've never known how I feel about that. As we know, innocent men and women have died throughout history. But when you have a man like Kenneth, who *will* kill again… I don't know what I believe."

"I'm just glad it isn't up to me," Jackson told her. "But you're right. With Kenneth, things could have gone horribly wrong at the bank. Billy and Cassie would have probably been killed once Kenneth and he slipped through the tunnels with the money. I wonder if Elise ever suspected that Kenneth would kill her, too, once he had the money, and she met up with him for her half. Anyway, thanks to the captain, we solved two murders, a kidnapping, and Billy will get some help instead of a prison sentence."

"Thanks to David. Jackson, I want to find him today."

"And we will. Don't worry, we're not going in to work. Bruce and Alex will be in the office watching over our agents in the field and handling whatever else needs doing. Okay?"

"A plan."

It started with their morning: breakfast with the kids.

And it was always wonderful to be with them, taking care of the dogs—their living pet *and* their ghost dog—and realize how incredibly lucky they were.

And every time they helped others…

It just made life better.

Soon enough, the kids were off, and while they had met and adopted Corby during a case when they learned that he had the strange thread of DNA that allowed him to see and speak with the dead, he was living a normal life, going to school, enjoying family time…just being a kid.

But when that very precious morning was over, Angela looked at Jackson and asked him, "Okay, how do we go about finding David?"

"Well, my love, this time, *I've* been doing some research," Jackson told her.

And thus it was that they headed to Arlington Cemetery.

"In 1948, Harry Truman desegregated the military," Jackson said as they walked through the hallowed ground. "Of course, David survived long after the Civil War, so he's in Section 23. I don't know why—"

"He's saying goodbye to friends today, you think?" Angela asked.

"I do. He's been here for a very long time. He didn't need to stay to help a family member; his children, grand-children, and great-grandchildren lived good lives. I think he's wondered why he's been here so long and…"

Naturally, they ran into a few other spirits, nodding and seeing them smile as they passed. There were and had been others in the world with the gift or curse of seeing the dead, of course, but it wasn't that common. So, the ghosts viewed them with smiles and curiosity.

They saw a man dressed in a chief petty officer's naval uniform, and Jackson paused to ask him about David.

The ghost of the World War II vet pointed him out.

David was there shaking hands with old friends.

But he saw them and smiled broadly, hurrying toward them and giving Angela a ghostly hug before shaking Jackson's hand.

"I can feel it. I can feel it's today," David told them. "And…well, I know. Somehow, I just know I'll see my wife and go to a place where all souls have learned to love and be together, and none of the petty problems of Earth exist. Sorry, I'm just, well, I'm just ready."

"We thought so," Jackson told him.

"And I'm sorry. I can't talk long. I need to…"

"Go, go," Angela told him. "David, thank you. We love you."

David paused for just a second and smiled. "Keep at it, no matter what others say and do. Keep at providing good-ness for everyone. The more who do, the better it becomes."

Then, he left.

There was a beautiful tree near the section, and David hurried to it and lifted his face to the sky.

And it came.

It wasn't a bolt of shocking light; it seemed rather gentle. A glow that slowly came like white mist in the air.

It encompassed the smiling man.

And, seconds later, the spirit of Captain David Clancy was gone.

Jackson looked at Angela and smiled.

"'All's well that ends well,'" he quoted.

And she knew that to be true.

# When Irish Eyes Are Haunting

Krewe of Hunters
By Heather Graham


Devin Lyle and Craig Rockwell are back, this time to a haunted castle in Ireland where a banshee may have gone wild—or maybe there's a much more rational explanation—one that involves a disgruntled heir, murder, and mayhem, all with that sexy light touch Heather Graham has turned into her trademark style.

----------

Chapter One

"Ah, you can hear it in the wind, you can, the mournful cry of the banshee!" Gary Duffy—known as Gary the Ghost—exclaimed with wide eyes, his tone low, husky and haunting along with the sound of the crackling fire. "It's a cry so mournful and so deep, you can feel it down into your bones. Indeed. Some say she's the spirit of a woman long gone who's lost everyone dear in her life; some say she is one of the fairy folk. Some believe she is a death ghost, and come not to do ill, but to ease the way of the dying, those leaving this world to enter the next. However she is known, her cry is a warning that 'tis time for a man to put his affairs in order, and kiss his loved ones good-bye, before taking that final journey that is the fate of all men. And women," he added, looking around at his audience. "Ah, and believe me! At Castle Karney, she's moaned and cried many a time, many a time!"

*Yes! Just recently*, Devin Lyle thought.

Very recently.

Gary spoke well; he was an excellent storyteller, more of a performer than a guide. He had a light and beautiful brogue that seemed to enhance his words as well and an ability to speak with a deep tone that carried, yet still seemed to be something of a whisper.

All in the tour group were enthralled as they watched him—even the youngest children in the group were silent.

But then, beyond Gary's talents, the night—offering a nearly full moon and a strange, shimmering silver fog—lent itself to storytelling and ghostly yarns. As did the lovely and haunting location where Gary spun his tales.

The group sat around a campfire that burned in an ancient pit outside the great walls of Castle Karney, halfway between those walls and St. Patrick's of the Village—the equally ancient church of Karney, said to have been built soon after the death of Ireland's patron saint. A massive graveyard surrounded the church; the Celtic crosses, angels, cherubs, and more, seemed to glow softly in a surreal shade of pearl beneath the moon. That great orb itself was stunning, granting light and yet shrouded in the mist that shimmered over the graveyard, the castle walls, and down to embrace the fire itself—and Gary the Ghost—in surreal and hypnotic beauty.

Gary's tour was thorough.

They'd already visited the castle courtyard, the cliffs, the church, and the graveyard, learning history and legends along the way.

The fire pit they now gathered around had been used often in the centuries that came before—many an attacking lord or general had based his army here, just outside the walls. They had cooked here, burned tar here for assaults, and stood in the light and warmth of the blaze to stare at the castle walls and dream of breeching them.

The walls were over ten feet thick. An intrepid Karney—

alive at the time of William the Conqueror—had seen to it that the family holding was shored up with brick and stone.

"The night is still now," Gary said, his voice low and rich. "But listen if you will when the wind races across the Irish Sea. And you'll hear the echo of her wail, on special nights, aye, the heart-wrenching cry of the banshee!"

Gary—Devin knew from her cousin, Kelly—was now the full-time historian, curator, and tour director at Castle Karney. She'd learned a lot from him, but, naturally, she'd known a lot already from family lore. Kelly Karney was her cousin and Devin had been to Castle Karney once before.

The Karney family had held title to the property since the time of St. Patrick. Despite bloodshed and wars, and multiple invasions first by Vikings and then British monarchs, they'd held tenaciously to the property. So tenaciously that fifteen years ago—to afford the massive property along with repairs and taxes—they had turned it into a fashionable bed and breakfast, touted far and wide on tourist sites as a true experience as well as a vacation.

Gary, with his wonderful ability to weave a tale, was part of the allure—as if staying in a castle with foundations and a great hall begun in the early part of the fifth century was not enough!

But Gary had gained fame in international guidebooks. While the Karney family had employed him first for the guests of the B&B, they'd always opened the tours to visitors who came to the village and stayed anywhere there—or just stopped by for the tour.

"Indeed! Here, where the great cliffs protected the lords of Karney from any assault by the Irish Sea, where the great walls stood tall against the slings, rams, arrows, and even canon of the enemy, the banshees wail is known to be heard. Throughout the years, 'twas heard each night before the death of the master of the house. Sometimes, they say, she cried to help an elderly lord make his way to the great castle in the sky. Yet she may cry for all, and has cast her mournful wail into the air for many a Karney, master or no. Saddest still, was the wailing of the banshee the night before the English knight, Sir Barry Martin, burst in to kidnap the Lady Brianna. He made his way through their primitive sewer lines of the day, thinking the castle would fall if he but held her, for she was a rare beauty and beloved of Declan, master of Karney Castle. Sir Martin made his way to the master's chambers, where he took the lady of the house, but Declan came upon him. Holding the Lady Brianna before Declan, Sir Martin slew her with his knife. In turn, Lord Declan rushed Sir Martin, and died himself upon the same knife—but not until he'd skewered Sir Martin through with his sword! It was a sad travesty of love and desire, for it was said Sir Martin coveted the Lady Brianna for himself, even as he swore to his men it was a way to breech the castle walls. While that left just a wee babe as heir, the castle stood, for Declan's mighty steward saw to it that the men fought on, rallying in their master's name. Aye, and when you hear the wind blow in now—like the high, crying wail of the banshee—they say you can see Brianna and her beloved. Karney's most famous ghosts are said to haunt the main tower. Through the years, they've been seen, Brianna and her Declan—separately, so they say, ever trying to reach one another and still stopped by the evil spirit of Sir Barry Martin!"

There was a gasp in the crowd. A pretty young woman turned to the young man at her side. "Oh! We're staying at Karney Castle!" she said. "And the main hall is just so hauntingly—haunted!"

"Ahha!" Gary said, smiling. "Hauntingly haunted! Aye, that it is!"

"We're staying there, too!" said an older woman.

"Ah, well, then, a number of you are lucky enough to be

staying at the castle," Gary said. "Ten rooms and suites she lets out a night! Be sure to listen—and keep good watch. Maybe you'll see or hear a ghost—there are many more, of course. It's been a hard and vicious history, you know. Of course, you need not worry if ya be afraid of ghosts—while the main tower is most known to be haunted, Brianna tends to roam the halls of the second floor, and that's where only the family stays."

Devin felt a hand on her shoulder and heard a gentle whisper at her ear. "You, my love. Have you seen Brianna?"

It was Rocky—Craig Rockwell, the love of her life, seated by her side, their knees touching. And it was the kind of whisper that made her feel a sweet warmth sear through her, teasing her senses.

Rocky was her husband of three days.

But though she smiled, she didn't let the sensual tease streak as far as it might. Oddly enough, his question was serious; partially because they were staying in the old master's suite, since they were family, through marriage—Rocky, through her. Devin, because her mother's sister April had long ago married Seamus Karney, youngest brother of the Karney family.

His question was also partially serious because they were who they were themselves—and what they did for a living, rather strange work, really, because it was the kind that could never be left behind.

She and Rocky had been together since a bizarre series of murders in Salem. Devin owned a cottage there, inherited from a beloved great aunt. Rocky had grown up in nearby Marblehead and had—technically—been part of the case since he'd been in high school. As an adult, he'd also been part of the FBI—and then part of an elite unit within the FBI, the Krewe of Hunters.

Devin had been—and still was—a creator of children's

books. But, she'd found herself part of the case as well, nearly a victim.

Somehow, in the midst of it all, they'd grown closer and closer—despite a somewhat hostile beginning. As they'd found their own lives in danger, they'd discovered that their natural physical attraction began to grow—and then they found they desperately loved one another and were, in many ways, a perfect match. Not perfect—nothing was perfect. But she loved Rocky and knew that he loved her with an equal passion and devotion.

*That was*, she thought, *as perfect as life could ever get.*

And, she'd discovered, she was a "just about as perfect as you were going to get" candidate for being a part of the Krewe as well. That had meant nearly half a year—pretty grueling for her, really—in the FBI Academy, but she'd come through and now she was very grateful.

Rocky had never told her what she should or shouldn't do. The choice had been hers, but she believed he was pleased with her position—it allowed them to work together, which was important since they traveled so much on cases. While the agency allowed marriages and relationships among employees, they usually had to be in different units. Not so with the Krewe. In the Krewe, relationships between agents aided in their pursuits.

While Devin had never known she'd wanted to be in law enforcement before the events in Salem, she felt now that she could never go back. She belonged in the Krewe because she did have a special talent—one shared by all those in the unit.

When they *chose* to be seen, she—like the others—had the ability to see the dead.

And speak with them.

It wasn't a talent she'd had since she'd been a child. It was one she had discovered when bodies had started piling up after she returned to live in Salem. The victim of a long ago persecution had found her, seeking help for those being murdered in the present in an age-old act of vengeance.

She still wrote her books, gaining ideas from her work. And being with the Krewe made her feel that she was using herself in the best way possible—helping those in need. She'd never wanted the world to be evil. And the world wasn't evil—just some people in it.

She did have to admit that her life had never seemed so complete. But, of course, that was mainly because she woke up each morning with Rocky at her side. And she knew that no matter how many years went by, she would love waking to his dark green eyes on her, even when his auburn hair grayed—or disappeared entirely. She loved Rocky—everything about him. He was one of the least self-conscious people she had ever met. He towered over her five-nine by a good six inches and was naturally lean but powerfully built, and yet totally oblivious to his appearance. Of course, he took his work very seriously and that meant time in a gym several days every week. Now, of course, she had to take to the gym every week herself.

Rocky was just much better at the discipline.

*Better at every discipline*, she thought dryly.

And also so compassionate, despite all that he'd seen in the world. When her cousin had called her nervously, begging her to come to Ireland, Rocky had been quick to tell Devin that yes, naturally, Adam Harrison and Jackson Crow—the founder and Director Special Agent of their unit, respectively—would give them leave to do so. And it had all worked out well, really, because they'd toyed with the idea of a wedding—neither wanted anything traditional, large, or extravagant—and they'd made some tentative plans, thinking they'd take time after and head for a destination like Bermuda.

They chose not to put off the wedding; in fact, they

pushed it up a bit. And instead of Bermuda or the Caribbean, they headed to Ireland.

A working honeymoon might not be ideal. Still, they'd been living together for six months before they married, so it wasn't really what some saw as a traditional honeymoon anyway. And, St. Patrick's Day was March 17th, just three days away from their landing on the Emerald Isle that noon. Her cousin, Kelly Karney, had promised amazing festivities, despite the recent death of Kelly's uncle, Collum Karney— the real reason they had come.

*A heart attack, plain and simple.*

*Then why was Collum discovered after the screeching, terrible howl of the banshee with the look of horror upon his face described by Brendan?*

"They say," Gary the Ghost intoned, his voice rich and carrying across the fire, and yet low and husky as well, "that Castle Karney carries within her very stone the heart and blood of a people, the cries of their battles, the lament of those lost, indeed, the cry of dead and dying…and the banshee come to greet them. Ah, yes, she's proven herself secure. 'Castle Karney in Karney hands shall lie, 'til the moon goes dark by night and the banshee wails her last lament!' So said the brave Declan Karney, just as the steel of his enemy's blade struck his flesh!"

Devin turned to look up at the castle walls.

Castle Karney.

Covered in time, rugged as the cliffs she hugged, and… Even as Devin looked at the great walls, it seemed that a shadow fell over them to embrace them, embrace Karney. A chill settled over her as she looked into the night, blinking. The shadow as dark and forbidding as the…

As the grave.

As Gary said, as old as time, and the caress of the banshee herself.

# About Heather Graham

*New York Times* and *USA Today* bestselling author, Heather Graham, majored in theater arts at the University of South Florida. After a stint of several years in dinner theater, back-up vocals, and bartending, she stayed home after the birth of her third child and began to write. Her first book was with Dell, and since then, she has written over two hundred novels and novellas including category, suspense, historical romance, vampire fiction, time travel, occult and Christmas family fare.

She is pleased to have been published in approximately twenty-five languages. She has written over 200 novels and has 60 million books in print. She has been honored with awards from booksellers and writers' organizations for excellence in her work, and she is also proud to be a recipient of the Silver Bullet Award from the International Thriller Writers and was also awarded the prestigious Thriller Master in 2016. She is also a recipient of the Lifetime Achievement Award from RWA and *Strand* magazine. Heather has had books selected for the Doubleday Book Club and the Literary Guild, and has been quoted, interviewed, or featured in such publications as The Nation, Redbook, Mystery Book Club, *People* and *USA Today* and appeared on many newscasts including *Today*, *Entertainment Tonight* and local television.

Heather loves travel and anything that has to do with the water and is a certified scuba diver. She also loves ballroom dancing. Each year she hosts a ball or dinner theater raising money for the Pediatric Aids Society and in 2006 she hosted the first Writers for New Orleans Workshop to benefit the stricken Gulf Region. She is also the founder of "The Slush Pile Players," presenting something that's "almost like entertainment" for various conferences and benefits. Married since high school graduation and the mother of five, her greatest love in life remains her family, but she also believes her career has been an incredible gift, and she is grateful every day to be doing something that she loves so very much for a living.

For more info, please stop by on Facebook or visit her web page: theoriginalheathergraham.com

# Also from Heather Graham

*The Stalking*
*Seeing the Darkness*
*Deadly Touch*
*Dreaming Death*
*Horror-Ween*
*The Best Christmas Ever*
*Sound of Darkness*
*Aura of Night*
*Voice of Fear*

## OTHER BOOKS BY HEATHER GRAHAM

*A Dangerous Game*
*Flawless*
*A Perfect Obsession*
*Let the Dead Sleep*
*Waking the Dead*
*Night of the Wolves*
*Night of the Vampires*
*Bride of the Night*
*The Keepers*
*Ghost Shadow*
*Ghost Night*
*Ghost Moon*
*Ghost Walk*
*Haunted*
*The Presence*
*The Vision*
*The Dead Room*
*The Séance*
*The Death Dealer*
*Nightwalker*
*Unhallowed Ground*
*The Killing Edge*
*Home in Time for Christmas*

*Dust to Dust*
*Deadly Night*
*Deadly Harvest*
*Deadly Gift*
*The Last Noel*
*Blood Red*
*Kiss of Darkness*
*The Island*
*Killing Kelly*
*Dead on the Dance Floor*
*Picture Me Dead*
*Hurricane Bay*
*A Season of Miracles*
*Never Sleep with Strangers*
*Eyes of Fire*
*Slow Burn*
*Danger in Numbers*
*Crimson Summer*

# Discover More Blue Box Press authors and their amazing stories…

*Go to www.TheBlueBoxPress.com for more information.*

Dylan Allen
Jennifer L. Armentrout
Kristen Ashley
Xio Axelrod
Steve Berry
Lexi Blake
Audrey Carlan
Marie Force
C. W. Gortner
Heather Graham
Donna Grant
Larissa Ione
Suzanne M. Johnson
J. Kenner
Randy Susan Meyers
Jennifer Probst
Kristen Proby
Christopher Rice
M.J. Rose
Kennedy Ryan
J.R. Ward

# On Behalf of Blue Box Press,
Liz Berry and Jillian Stein would like to thank ~

Steve Berry
Benjamin Stein
Kim Guidroz
Chelle Olson
Tanaka Kangara
Ann-Marie Nieves
Grace Wenk
Asha Hossain
Chris Graham
Jessica Saunders
Stacey Tardif
Suzy Baldwin
Dylan Stockton
Richard Blake
and Simon Lipskar

9 781968 707590